NOVEMBER 22, 1963

NOVEMBER 22,1963

ADAM BRAVER

a novel

TinHouseBooks

This is a work of fiction. Names, characters, places, and incidents either are
the product of the author's imagination or are used fictitiously.

Published by Tin House Books, Portland, Oregon, and New York, New York
Distributed to the trade by Publishers Group West, 1700 Fourth St.,
Berkeley, CA 94710, www.pgw.com

Library of Congress Cataloging-in-Publication Data

Braver, Adam, 1963-
November 22, 1963 / Adam Braver. -- 1st U.S. ed.
p. cm.
ISBN 978-0-9802436-2-8
1. Kennedy, John F. (John Fitzgerald), 1917-1963--Assassination--Fiction.
2. Onassis, Jacqueline Kennedy, 1929-1994--Fiction. 3. Presidents--
Assassination--Fiction. 4. Political crimes and offenses--Fiction. I. Title.
PS3602.R39N68 2008
813'.6--dc22   2008020190
First U.S. edition 2008

ISBN 10: 0-9802436-2-9

Interior design by Laura Shaw, Inc.

Chapters from this book originally appeared in the following publications:
"Mrs. Kennedy Is Organizing Herself" in *Water-Stone Review*;
"The Science of Warmth" in *West Branch*; "Breaking and Crumbling
on the Seventeenth Floor" in *Harvard Review*; "The Oath of Office"
in *Ontario Review*; and "The Casket" in *Tin House*.

www.tinhouse.com

Printed in Canada

FOR NAT

*"I want minimum information given
with maximum politeness."*

—Jackie Kennedy

DRESSING IN THE HOTEL TEXAS

Some Facts.

When she moved into the White House, Jackie was a size 12.
When she left she was a size 8.

Coco Chanel used wool jersey for her suits, a fabric that previously had been reserved for men's underwear. She said it was the perfect material for creating both comfort and understatement.

Jackie demanded that her outfits have clean and compact lines.
The material should be firm in body, always holding its shape.

Jackie also popularized the bouffant hairdo, the pillbox hat, and large buttons that resembled gold coins.

Historically, the pillbox hat was a military headdress. In 1962 Halston designed the pillbox hat for Jackie. Halston became a household name; he no longer was Roy Frowick from Des Moines.

The *New York Times* once asked Jackie if she really spent $30,000 in couture shops on a single trip to Paris. "I couldn't spend that much," she answered, "unless I wore sable underwear." Always the partisan, Pat Nixon responded by saying she preferred American designers, that they are the best in the world. Nixon added, "I buy most of *my* clothes off the racks in different stores around Washington."

Pink.

Traditionally, white is a symbol of purity, while red connotes passion. When they're combined into pink, the color indicates gentleness. It also tends to symbolize new birth.

The Suite in the Hotel Texas.

Wanting to make Jack and Jackie's stay as memorable as possible, a group of Fort Worth patrons arranged to have a mini art exhibit hung in the presidential suite at the Hotel Texas. Van Gogh. Monet. Picasso. The patrons even went so far as to create an exhibit catalog. Because they didn't arrive until nearly midnight, neither Jack nor Jackie even noticed it. It didn't get their full attention until morning.

Readying for Dallas.

The staff told her it would be cool that day, but a Texan's presumption of cold is still hot by any other standard. From the window of the suite at the Hotel Texas, the weather over Fort Worth seemed unassuming, with just a little bit of rain. Still, it was November, and the area was prone to tornados and other meteorological oddities. It occurred to her that maybe she should have packed something lighter. A fabric that breathes. Already hers looked too heavy for the climate. Dallas might be colder, which would make the outfit seem a little more practical. Glancing out at the shifting Texas sky, she found it hard to imagine that the weather could be predicted with such confidence. Yet there was no choice but to take them at their word. She had only the wool suit.

Simple.

She had kept a low profile over the past few months, since Patrick's death. The grief had overwhelmed her in a way that she had never known before, consuming her to the point where the insides of her bones ached, and her thoughts, usually sharp and aware, were deadened, as though each neuron had been stepped on and flattened.

Nobody had pressured her to take this trip, but the Party people were thrilled—tickets and donations for the Texas events skyrocketed when word leaked that the first lady would be coming out West too. The thought of returning to a normal life sounded good. She would work hard on the reelection. Focus her energies on the campaign. And she would travel lightly. Simply. Try to reduce the attention on her. No new clothes. Maybe one dress for cocktail parties, and a day dress and a coat. No maids. Only her secretary, Mary Gallagher, to help with the packing after each stop. And Jackie would even do her own hair.

It was all meant to be simple. A gradual reentry into the living.

Speaking Spanish.

They'd been in Houston for a dinner before taking off later that evening for Fort Worth. It was an appreciation event for Congressman Albert Thomas, a showcase in front of more than three thousand attendees at the Sam Houston Coliseum, all ponying up money to encourage Thomas to seek another term. But Jack's people had discovered a free hour in the schedule, and, out of the more than one thousand solicitations, the president accepted an invitation from Paul Andow of the League of United Latin American Citizens.

At the event, Jack decided to take the backseat. He introduced Jackie to the crowd, where she delivered a speech in near-perfect Spanish, charming the audience with her quietly composed voice.

She felt confident on the podium. For a moment completely forgetting the loss. Finding her comfort in the anonymity of another language.

In the Bedroom of the Hotel Texas: Part One.

On the morning of November 22 at the Hotel Texas, Jackie decided to skip the scheduled 8:45 speech in the hotel parking lot, instead opting to meet up with Jack at the chamber of commerce breakfast in the ballroom. She was tired, and a feeling of uncertainty had come over her again. She just wanted some extra time. To gather herself, remind herself that everything would be okay.

She stood in front of the mirror, stroking her hip bone. She was not as delicate as people made her out to be. Her body was a structure made to withstand disaster. She was no pane of glass. Even at twenty-seven, when their first child, Arabella, died at birth, Jackie had relied on poise to see her through, standing firm at the funeral in Newport while others fell apart for her. But Patrick's death had shown her the vulnerability of the world. And since his passing, even in the strongest of moments, she'd been aware of the fragility of the ground where she walked. These days, for the most part, she could expect the feeling to pass. But every once in a while, she found that she needed to sit down. Put her feet up. She was afraid that a single step might shatter everything, splinter the world into millions of tiny fractures.

She glanced over at the matching pink skirt and jacket on a hanger before turning back to her reflection. Her body looked both young and tired. Ruined but with potential. Carefully, she laid the clothes across the dressing chair so they wouldn't wrinkle, smoothing the skirt with her hand. Stripped down to just her slip and bra, Jackie sat on the edge of the bed, still watching herself, like a paper doll undressed.

The Bubbletop.

There was a moment when the bubbletop was considered. In a brief conversation with Jackie's press secretary, Pam Turnure, Jack had asked whether she thought they should put the transparent roof on the limousine. There was some discussion about Jackie's strength for the upcoming trip, and about her keeping her mettle, but the real question came down to Jackie's hair, and whether the wind might damage her hairdo. After some consideration, Pam looked up at him and said, "Maybe we should use the bubbletop," and, as though there had been no consideration, he shot back immediately, "That's semi-satisfactory. If you're going out to see the people, then they should be able to see you."

In the Bedroom of the Hotel Texas: Part Two.

From behind the bedroom door, Secret Service Agent Clint Hill knocked to inform Jackie that they would need to leave the suite in five minutes. The president was already in the ballroom and had sent up for her.

Jackie looked once at the pink suit, still wondering if it was too heavy for a Texas day. Either way, she figured, she'd be out of it by dinner. The suit was a strangely enchanting shade of pink, without the usual candylike artifice. It looked alive to her in a botanical way, as though vines and stems should be connected to it. She buttoned her blouse and stepped into her skirt. The jacket fit freely and comfortably. From the closet she took out a hatbox with Halston's latest, a perfectly matching pillbox. She placed it on her head with ceremonial delicacy.

The Eyes of Texas.

In the kitchen, she stood alongside agents Howard and Hill. She couldn't count how many hotel kitchens she had passed through during these political years. Aromas lingering, gas flames burning, tubs and tins and ramekins filled with spices and sauces, yet the room eerily void of all the people who, for security reasons, had temporarily been ushered out. Always a sense of aftermath.

The pots hanging from the wall shone. Knowing the president would be walking through, the hotel management always ensured that all kitchen items were polished. Each way she looked, Jackie saw her reflection staring back at her. Sometimes flattened and distorted. Other times so real she had to feel for her face. But with the final glance she saw herself as she looked in pictures. Poised. Dignified. A pure form of sophistication. Someone who controlled fortune.

Agent Hill gave the signal, at which Howard gently touched Jackie on the elbow, saying, *We need to go*, and walked beside her through the kitchen, past the cluster of kitchen staff huddled in an office space (the Mexican dishwashers pushed farthest against the back wall), and to the swinging door. Just before it opened, Jackie peered through the porthole at the tables full of people all craning their necks to see what was going on behind them. And among them was Jack. He looked boyish. For one brilliant moment, unpresidential. He glanced to the bandstand in anticipation, and then back to the doors as the orchestra struck up the first note of "The Eyes of Texas Are Upon You." Hill swung open the doors with the first downbeat and Ray Buck's booming introduction, and Jackie walked in, floating, almost ghostly.

The audience rose to its feet as she walked to the head table. A lone pink flower among stiffly swaying grasses. Jack also stood, looking at her. Watching her. And even more than the love in his eyes, she saw the pride. At the table he took her hands and brought her in for a kiss on the cheek. "My pink rose," he whispered.

At the podium, Ray Buck presented Jack with a genuine Texas cowboy hat, followed by a pair of cowboy boots. Although Jack admired and considered the gifts, he didn't put on the hat.

After a few brief thank-yous, Jack looked out over the room and then down to Jackie. "Two years ago," he began, "I introduced myself in Paris by saying that I was the man who had accompanied Mrs. Kennedy to Paris. I am getting somewhat the same sensation as I travel around Texas. Nobody wonders what Lyndon and I wear."

Although she hadn't wanted to stand out on this trip—keep it simple—Jack's comment was comforting, bringing her back to a familiar place, where she understood the order and the rules.

She didn't pay attention to the rest of his remarks. Texas being Texas, he focused the speech on defense, and spoke specifically about Fort Worth's air-defense industry. He was his usual captivating self. Glancing around the room, Jackie saw each member of the audience looking up at Jack, locked in, as though he were speaking only to them.

After finishing his speech, he stepped down and took her hand, lifted her from her seat, and together they walked down the aisle, smiling while shaking hands, all the way into the kitchen, where the hotel staff were again corralled hurriedly out of the way and into the office.

Laughing It Off.

The *Dallas Morning News* had run an ad on page two by a zealot named Bernard Weissman. It was a full page, with the bolt-

ing headline WELCOME MR. KENNEDY TO DALLAS, followed by a series of pointed questions, each bulleted by the
word WHY. Every sentence alluded to the president having
Communist interests at stake, with the final point being, "WHY
have you scrapped the Monroe Doctrine in favor of the 'Spirit
of Moscow'?" and closing with "MR. KENNEDY, as citizens of
these United States of America, we DEMAND answers to these
questions, and want them NOW." Mr. Weissman, on behalf of
the "American Fact-Finding Committee," signed the ad.

Standing by the sitting room window in the suite, Jack said,
"It doesn't quite make you want to rush off to Dallas, does it
now?" Although his back was to the room, Jack's comment was
directed to Kenny O'Donnell. Special assistant. Closest advisor.
Protector. It seemed all Jack's remarks went to him.

"Well, at least it isn't the National Indignation Committee,"
Kenny replied. "They're the ones who started the Adlai
Stevenson incident, if you remember. Also called Lyndon the
Smiling Judas."

"I'm not sure I've ever seen Lyndon smile," Jack said.

Kenny laughed, along with some other aides. "Well, you
watch out for that National Indignation Committee, Mr.
President. They'll rock you harder than they did Stevenson."

"Well, we'll find out shortly, won't we? Then it's over and out
of the way. Leave them to Lyndon."

"Speaking of Lyndon," Kenny said. He reminded Jack that
they needed to go over to the Johnson suite, as Lyndon's sister
and brother-in-law had arranged to stop by, hoping to meet the
president.

"Maybe," Jack said, "Lyndon ought to be reintroducing himself to Senator Yarborough instead, so in the future we don't
have to bother with these thrill rides."

Serious.

Jackie sat in a plush, mustard-colored chair, looking out the window, trying not to listen to the conversation, as some of the others joined in with the Dallas jokes. In half the window she could see herself reflected. In the other half she saw the clouds. They looked as though they were thinning. The day seemed to be getting a little brighter. It turned her suit pinker, and it made the material feel heavier.

She knew everybody was riding high from last night in Houston and from this morning's breakfast, but she didn't like hearing them joke about the threats. The fact was that Dallas was unwelcoming to northern Democrats. The men in the room could make all the cracks they wanted about Jack getting the Stevenson treatment, but Stevenson hadn't found it so funny when he was in Dallas to speak at the U.N. Day Program, getting smacked over the head while a mob attacked his car, chanting slogans about tearing down the U.N. "I don't want to send them to jail," Stevenson had said. "I want to send them to school."

She thought to protest their casualness, tell Jack and Kenny, and everybody else who was laughing along, that this ought to be taken seriously. Acknowledge the tension. But she knew they would only attribute it to her nerves and her recovery. Treat her as though she were infirm, with kind and gentle touches on the elbows and overextended offers of water or juice, apologizing for being so insensitive while swallowing down their laughter, afraid of her fragility.

She really wanted to say something. But was it best to stay quiet? Maybe she was imposing her anxieties upon them.

If they just would see.

Take this seriously. That was all. It's too easy to laugh your-self into tragedy.

On to Dallas.

Jack had been on the phone for some time. One call after the other. Donors. Local politicians. Luminaries. Patrons of the arts. Thanking them for their support. Agreeing with their causes. Saying that Mrs. Kennedy was doing much better now, and that he certainly would pass on their prayers and their words. He had finished up a call, the receiver still cradled against his neck, two fingers holding down the hook switch, when he whispered up at Kenny, "When do we need to be in Lyndon's room?"

"Five minutes ago."

"Time for one more call?"

Kenny shook his head. "Maybe from Dallas later."

"If we make it."

"Don't worry," Kenny said. "This whole trip will be over before we know it." He then announced that the motorcade would leave upon the president's return from the suite. Finally, they'd be relieved of the Hotel Texas and press on toward Dallas.

"And then home, I hope," Jack said. He walked over to Jackie. She was pacing. Looking at the art on the walls. They may hang cow skulls from every spare nail in this state, but when it comes to taste, even the Texas socialites turned to the Europeans. "I'll be back shortly," he told her. "Momentarily. You know how these things are." He said he wanted her to rest up. Save her energy for Dallas. There was a long day ahead.

Jackie reached out, taking his hand. She started to speak, but stopped. It was just all the joking about Dallas. Even though it was just talk, it was making her nervous, and she wondered if he were nervous too. You never could tell with him. And she wondered if he remembered what she said to him the night the baby died, only two days old. Feeling decimated, stripped bare of all control and everything she knew, she had looked up at Jack and told him that the one thing she couldn't bear would be to lose him. And he had held her, told her he had no plans to go anywhere. She hadn't repeated herself, instead squeezed him tighter.

"Is everything okay?" he asked.

She drew in a deep breath. Adjusted the hair falling from under her hat. She'd even managed to keep her eyes clear and dry. "This suit just feels so heavy right now. You know that feeling, Jack? That feeling like you've been carrying something forever. That's how this feels. Eleven o'clock and I feel as though I've been wearing it all day, and will wear it forever. That's all."

"You look stunning."

"The weather outside. It's so . . . Maybe I should change."

With one foot stepping toward the door, he held on to her hand. He turned to her, locking her in with the same mesmeric charm that had entranced every member of the earlier audience. "No," he said, "I want people to remember how beautiful you are today. I hope they always will remember you in this dress. A pink rose."

One More Fact.

More than forty years later, the pink dress remains boxed up at the National Archives in "courtesy storage" for the Kennedy family.

BODY AND BLOOD

HE WAS JUST A BARBER'S BOY. Not intended to amount to anything but the same-old in Cleburne, Texas, some thirty-seven miles away from Fort Worth and a million miles away from everywhere else. And when you're making barely forty dollars a week, and you've got a wife and a child, you look up one day knowing you can do yourself better. So you go to Dallas after your cousin Jim tells you Dallas is your future and the Dallas PD is hiring. This is as brave as anything one could imagine, because you and your family are little-town people. And before he knows, it's 1963 and nine and a half years have passed and he's no longer a young fellow from Cleburne but a bona fide Dallas man, and on the motorcycle squad, and there are three others who get the call, and when he goes to bed on the evening of November 21, how could he possibly sleep? Not toss and turn? Wouldn't the thoughts pound through his head like a wrecking ball on a pendulum, until pretty soon he'd want to yell out, *I'm just a barber's boy?*

The barber's boy who'd come from Cleburne is named Bobby Hargis, and he waits at Love Field for the president's plane to arrive, pushing at the creases in his slacks, grinding the toe of his boot into the tarmac, and adjusting his helmet. The town he'd been raised in, come to at age seven from Rio Vista when his father passed, was named in honor of the heroic Confederate general Patrick Cleburne, born in County Cork, Ireland, and come to the United States in 1849. Cleburne was working as a lawyer in Tennessee when he enlisted in the Confederate army out of loyalty to the Southern people who had taken in this Irishman as one of their own. Patrick Cleburne skyrocketed to being one of the most respected generals, and then fell just as quickly in 1864, when, recognizing the lack in the Confederate army, he proposed emancipating slaves and enlisting them in the fight. Jefferson Davis himself put an end to that kind of talk, and later in the year Cleburne was shot in the gut on a battleground in Tennessee, charging in an assault he never believed to be wise. Patrick Cleburne was the highest-ranking Irishman in an American army. It's amazing how histories can converge at a single point on a world that spins around so many times.

When Bobby arrived in Dallas he worked on the patrol unit. It was there he got to know most of the people he would know, including J. D. Tippit. Tippit was already on the force when Bobby joined, working as a patrolman. The two of them formed a friendship that extended beyond the police family. They'd hang out after their shifts. Often working together off duty at the drive-in on Illinois, lingering between changing posts and shooting the breeze, talking about guys like Bailey and everybody else they knew in common. A couple of kindred boys, both come to Dallas as small-town folks hoping to make a better life for themselves and their families. Then, in 1957, the department put out a call for motorcycle officers, and Bobby thought, *Why not?* After he put in his request, one of his chiefs called to ask, *Still interested?* and Bobby said, *Yes,* and the chief said, *Then report to work day after tomorrow in your civilian clothes,* and Bobby said, *Okay.*

— — — — —

When you talked with him by phone, Bobby was polite. Thoughtful. He spoke slowly, and reminded you he was old, and that some of the things he used to know he didn't know so well anymore; he could always recite the motorcade stories clearly, but the other questions stopped him. Sometimes gave him pause. And there was a sense that he was surprised anybody cared about the in-between details. Like when you asked him what he did that night after the shooting. And he claimed not to remember, which was a little disappointing since you wanted that for the story you planned to tell. So you asked him what it was like waiting at Love Field, and he told you it was like any other day. Although the details were interesting, it was an emotional truth you were after, but there just wasn't one for him to recall. He had told you about getting called down to join the motorcycle squad, but again you wanted a different story, to know how he got the news that he'd be guarding Kennedy's car. You tried to make the question lighthearted, and put it to him this way: "And then one day you're getting a call that says, 'Bobby, guess what you're doing tomorrow?'" And there was a little silence on the receiver, and then a low, deep laugh before he drew out the word *Well*, and said, "That was just an assignment."

— — — — —

The anticipation starts in shudders, and soon it seems as though all of Love Field is trembling. As part of the motorcycle division, Bobby, Douglass, Billy Joe, and Chaney have escorted famous people from Love Field before. They know what to expect. But this is a different level of excitement, and a different level of seriousness. The giddiness of anticipation is tempered by the reality of the guest, and the fact that some people have made it known that Kennedy ought to stay out of Texas. Still, there are kooks everywhere. Kennedy's as welcome here as anybody else.

The sun's come out, and everyone feels the region getting just a little bit bigger, ready to welcome the Kennedys with a loud Dallas greeting, a hug that'll sink them deep in its bosom.

Sergeants. Captains. Chiefs. Lieutenants. Everybody from the department is present. Photographers load their cameras. Clusters of donors and dignitaries and local politicians mill and make small talk. Secret Service agents are littered all over. Hundreds of little flags are waving. And although the crowd is thick and deep and faceless, there are people who manage to stick out for no logical reason: a woman in a brown dress holding against her chest a magazine with Mrs. Kennedy on the cover; a child in horn-rimmed glasses who looks like he doesn't know why he's there; an old lady in a wheelchair planting herself at the head of the group, her face hawklike, waiting sentry.

The presidential limousine had been airlifted in the day before, and then spent the night heavily guarded in the garage under the main terminal. Now on the tarmac, the car waits to be filled with the governor and the president and both their wives. That car looks proud and it looks serious. You can smell the history burning right off it. It's all jacked up with platforms for Secret Service agents, the rear seat rising nearly a foot higher for a better view, and the whole vehicle a good yard or more longer than the everyday Lincoln Continental. The transparent roof panels that make the famed bubbletop have just been put in the trunk, now that the sun is peeking through the clouds.

Cruising Dallas in a convertible.

Black Ray-Bans.

She'll wave to the left side, he'll handle the right.

The Secret Service hoped the drizzle would turn to rain. A lousy day makes for a safer trip.

They look smaller than expected, coming down the airline stairs, framed by the blue nose of the 707. They're like orbs of light—he a dark blue ray, and she, soft pink. Coming closer, their faces become defined, and Mrs. Kennedy looks tired and cautious, watching her feet land on the next step, while the president's eyes twinkle to life when the first hand comes out to greet him. And then Mrs. Kennedy is handed a bouquet of roses, which almost blends with her suit, and soon they're both shaking hands with their audience on the way to the limousine. The president starts to seem larger and larger, as though gaining strength. Hollywood galloping into Dallas. Mrs. Kennedy, pausing to talk with the old woman in the wheelchair, seems more and more delicate—a strange collision of fragility and strength. And there are so many details to catalog. The wheel-chair woman's blue dress. A lace collar. A red blanket on her lap that matches Mrs. Kennedy's roses. But it all moves so fast. Bobby's already forgetting what's right before him.

He looks up to see the president a few feet away, working his way down the line, about to shake Bobby's hand. There are times in your life when no matter how much you've earned, you never really believe you've deserved it. Kennedy's grip is strong, and his smile is all movie-star charm. He looks at Bobby as though he recognizes something, and tells him, "I'm glad you're here. Thank you for being here." And although Bobby is a long way from Cleburne, Kennedy seems like something familiar from his past, a man who knows the value of a hand-shake and a gracious word. Who knows the good in people accepting you. In his mind, Bobby etches every word the president says to him.

— — — — —

"What would the guys in your father's barbershop have thought of Kennedy?" He paused and said, "I don't quite understand you." You stopped, unsure how to explain, realizing that although you'd had an agenda behind the question, you didn't really know what that agenda was, other than trying to find a new way into the story. You waited. Took a breath. Looked for the objectivity that felt as though it were slipping away. At something of a loss, you repeated the question. Said it a little louder, as if trying to bully a foreigner with English. He cut you off midsentence to say that he was only a boy when his father died, that was why they had left Rio Vista for Cleburne. So you reframed the question. "What about you? What did you think of Kennedy?" And he said, "Oh." Then there was a pause, and in that pause, across the transom, you could see his words starting to change shape, going from squares to ovals, and his whole tone brightened when he said that Kennedy "was like one of the preachers in my church that can hold your attention, and get you feeling exactly what he's saying."

— — — — —

In the limousine, Governor and Mrs. Connally sit one row ahead of the president, and Mrs. Kennedy takes her place to Jack's left, her little pink hat blooming against the sky. Kennedy leans forward to say something to the Connallys, and then hits his hand on the back of the seat, his laugh cutting through the din of Bobby's motorcycle.

Kennedy jerks back a little as the motorcade begins. Mrs. Kennedy waves to the entourage, her eyes looking downward, as though trapped.

On Cedar Springs Road, just barely out of the airport, the limousine moves at a crawl between the walls of spectators. Bobby tries to keep close to the car, but navigating the crowds takes him off center. Breaks his focus. Kennedy sits up, as though he's calling up to the driver, and like that, the limo stops.

Kennedy is not in the car.

Bobby slams on the brakes, unsure what is going on, and the Secret Service hot potato themselves all over the place, crouching and guarding, calling back and forth to one another, just about having a collective heart attack. It's only a split second that seems like forever until he sees that the president is just shaking hands, spotlighted in the sunshine breaking through the clouds.

— — — — —

You asked, "Is that the first time you sensed tension that day?" and Bobby tells you, "Well, when somebody else gets nervous, you're gonna get nervous too." But you wanted to know if that nervousness held, if it overtook the mood. You wanted a narrative. A broader part of the day that maybe he didn't see then. And so you widen the question, and ask if, upon reflection, there was a general sense of tension that permeated the day from the start, and although you're talking by telephone, you can see his head shake confidently as he says, "No, sir."

— — — — —

The route has been well publicized, even published in the morning paper. There's not a person in Dallas who doesn't know every inch of the motorcade's course, Bobby included. He follows it down Main toward Elm, trying to hug the limousine, keeping a vigilant eye on both Mrs. Kennedy and the boisterous crowd.

Most of the congestion is in Dealey Plaza, and Bobby can see that once they close in on the underpass, the road will open, and he'll be able to move into a better formation. But he's still not nervous. It's all going smoothly—the flags are streaming in streaks of red, white, and blue, and everybody is smiling and waving—and it makes him feel good to see the respect of his fellow Texans, because there was all that talk about hating Kennedy, but Bobby knew all along those were just small factions, and it wasn't even worth paying them any mind or attention, because there are always going to be small factions, and not a one ever deserves the mind or attention it's looking for.

Bobby can see the bottleneck breaking open a little farther up Elm. Nearly free. They'll be through the worst of it by the time they approach the Trade Mart. There's even a touch of breeze on his face that feels fresher. More open. He looks once at Mrs. Kennedy, seeing the same smile she's had on her face since leaving the airport, and then he looks away for a half second, and it's only a half second, but it's the sound that draws Bobby back.

— — — — —

You told him you weren't going to ask him to recount the shooting. *It must be difficult*, you explained, plus you've read other interviews he's given, gone through his Warren Commission testimony, to which he asked, "You read an interview with me?" His surprise seemed genuine. In truth (and though you wouldn't want to admit to it), avoiding the story has nothing to do with how difficult it might be for him. It's because you have a narrative in mind, and your conversation's main intent is to have a recorded witness for the details of the story. But no matter how much you'd planned to avoid it, suddenly the limousine turns on Elm toward the triple underpass at the same moment a hammer is being cocked on the sixth floor. And, that quickly, the story you weren't looking for is the story that is now taking place.

Hargis: I knew the shot didn't come from the front. It didn't come from underneath. Or from the side. It'd got to come from up above his right shoulder.

Interviewer: It must have been frightening.

Hargis: Your level of heartbeat race goes up. Your blood pressure goes up. Everything goes up.

Interviewer: What was going through your head?

Hargis: Just do what I was trained to do . . . If he'd wanted to, Oswald could've filled *me* full of holes. I didn't know where the shots was coming from.

— — — — —

They always want to know about the blood. Sam Stern, as assistant counsel on the Warren Commission, wants to know about the blood. In Dallas, gathering testimony for the report, Stern seems to break from the flat, just-the-facts questioning to ask Bobby about the blood. It almost suggests an innate understanding that facts alone aren't enough to make a story. He asks, "Did something happen to you personally in connection with the shot you have just described?"

Bobby replies, "You mean about the blood hitting me?" and Stern says, "Yes."

"Yes," Bobby answers back, in a reflexive affirmation. Then, following a semicolon pause, he explains that "when President Kennedy straightened back up in the car, the bullet hit him in the head, the one that killed him, and it seemed like his head exploded, and I was splattered with blood and brain, and kind of a bloody water. It wasn't really blood. And at that time the presidential car slowed down. I heard somebody say, 'Get going,' or 'get going' . . ."

Everybody wanted the story. They wanted the step by step, the moment when Bobby wiped the brain matter off his lip, where he was, what was going through his mind. But the truth of it is that nothing was going through his mind other than the white flash of instinct. There was not a pause in which he contemplated the fragility of life, or the mechanics of the human body, or the plausibility of the soul. It was just what he was *trained to do*. It was bullets flying, and the president's head exploding, and Connally maybe dead, and someone yelling, "Get going," and the limousine speeding off, and him jumping off his bike, looking everywhere and nowhere at once. Running through the crowd, sidestepping a weeping woman, and nearly leaping over a father lying atop his child. And back to his motorcycle to chase down the ghost assailant by the underpass, and then back to the School Book Depository, following a feeling, the way Kennedy was shot making him sense that that was the place where the "bullet come from," and he got there with several other police officers and was posted by a possible exit, where he waited and waited and waited until he was relieved of duty, never considering for a moment that there was part of Kennedy's brain filmed across his face.

But that's what they want to talk about. What they want to know. If he tasted it.

He was just a barber's boy. Nine and a half years out of Cleburne, and he's got a dream that will follow him nearly every night for most of his life. He'll be chasing Oswald, running and running but never quite able to catch him. Although his life moves forward and he stays on the job, he's always caught in that half second that rewinds and plays itself over and over again. And he can tell it so well now, almost say it with the distance that it deserves, but the one point where his voice still breaks is when he speaks of J. D. Tippit; his voice drops because he doesn't think of that day as one in which he found himself inside a story. It's a day when this barber's boy from Rio Vista had one of his best friends killed by the man who shot the president, just cruising his beat in Oak Cliff in car No. 10, nearly three miles away from the shooting, spotting Oswald, and pulling up to him on East Tenth to take a series of bullets in the chest, unloaded from Oswald's revolver. Bobby Hargis wasn't there to see that. But sometimes, like General Cleburne, you just can't fathom why people can't see the things you know to be right. Maybe that's when you stop asking questions and submit to the fact that what's been laid out behind you will forever be in front of you.

THE CASKET

A CASKET AND A COFFIN are not the same thing. A casket is four-sided, with the traditional squared shape, averaging about eighty-four inches in length and twenty-eight inches in diameter. A coffin is most recognizable from vampire movies, wide at the shoulders, slowly tapering at the feet. Funeral homes still carry coffins. They are referred to as "specialty items."

— — — — —

The Handley solid bronze casket was sold to the O'Neal Funeral Home in Dallas, Texas, on February 18, 1963, for a wholesale price of $1,031. It had a double-walled interior, something that would ensure protection from the geological pressures and shifts, as well as the day-to-day strains of the cemetery. It was top-of-the-line. But after the casket sat in storage for nine months, one wonders if Vernon O'Neal thought he might have made a bad purchase, overestimating the tastes of his higher-end clientele—or at least their willingness to invest that much in a casket. There must have been some secret relief when a call came in from Parkland Memorial Hospital with Secret Service Agent Roy Kellerman, saying, "Bring me your best available!"

— — — — —

Carolyn Hawkins's brother, Aubrey Rike, who went by the name of Al, was sitting at Parkland Memorial Hospital when the motorcade passed through Dealey Plaza. As an ambulance driver for O'Neal Funeral Home, Al and his rider, Peanuts McGuire, had been at the parade route earlier, sent down to Houston and Elm to pick up a man who had suffered a seizure across from the School Book Depository. They'd taken him over to Parkland, per O'Neal's contract with the city for ambulance services, and were standing around chatting when news of the shooting spread through the hospital almost as quickly as the president's car arrived.

Within moments the ER was swarmed. The stink of rushing bodies. Al found himself jammed against a wall, shoved up beside an agitated policeman who kept looking down at his feet while telling Al to stay put. He might be needed.

People ran chaotically. Newspapermen scurried for telephones. Elected officials milled. Congressmen. Senators. A general stood with a briefcase handcuffed to his wrist, as though he might blow the whole place to smithereens. Dallas PD. County PD. Secret Service. FBI. At least fifty people smashed right into the entrance, with a whole lot more spilling into the waiting room. Outside, hundreds of people crowded the barricade. Men with submachine guns guarded the glass entry doors. More and more kept arriving. Not enough air to feed them all.

After about a half hour, Secret Service Agent Kellerman approached. His arms folded across his chest, crumpling his customary dark suit. Falsely composed. A bubble ready to burst. He said Mr. O'Neal would be bringing a casket down shortly and would need both Al and Peanuts to be ready to assist with the necessary details. Kellerman said to wait for O'Neal right outside the trauma room. Maybe Al heard wrong? Misunderstood the part about the casket.

For Al Rike, the sense of history was overwhelming. His uncles Melvin and Leonard had driven the first ambulances in Dallas, and at one point Leonard had even opened up his own funeral home. Al had a sense for these kinds of things; he'd transported bodies back and forth as long as he could remember. But right now it felt as though the world had stopped, everything frozen in place, and he was the only one moving. It was so hectic that it felt slow. Like every movement mattered, engraving itself into the history books in real time.

Outside the trauma room, Al sat on top of a gurney pushed up against the wall. Legs dangling off the side. Peanuts paced the hall. Mr. O'Neal had arrived, but Kellerman advised O'Neal to keep the casket out of sight for the time being, so O'Neal hobnobbed, sticking close to the prominent types. All these people, and Al felt completely alone.

He was startled by a scraping sound. Next to him an agent wrestled with a metal folding chair. Then the first lady sat down, instinctively shrugging away the agent's guidance. Al tried not to look. Shifting on his gurney, he wiped cold sweat off his brow. Outside the trauma room with Mrs. Kennedy. In a metal folding chair?

Mrs. Kennedy's head turned slightly, her dark hair falling forward over her face. Al noticed her lips, taut and still, just parted enough for some air to get through. Nobody talked to her. Her husband lay behind the door while surgeons of all stature pretended to try to keep him alive. It was as if people were frightened of her. The agent had told her to sit and wait. So she sat and waited.

Al wished he were one of those people who knew the right things to say. She deserved the respect of comfort. A kind word. But his whole brain felt tongue-twisted. Just a twenty-five-year-old Texas boy who started his day by scooping up epileptics. It was enough for him just to keep his composure. So he took a cigarette from his pocket and lit it, inhaling slowly. Thinking up what he might say, and how he might say it.

Mrs. Kennedy uncrossed her legs and then recrossed them in the other direction. She looked right at Al. He was sick with nerves, but afraid to look away. "Do you have an extra?" she said. Her voice was quiet. Low and mechanical.

Al nearly dropped the butt, catching it on his bottom lip. He'd just bought a whole pack from the vending machine, but suddenly he couldn't remember what he did or didn't have.

"May I have a cigarette?" she said a little louder, although still just above a whisper.

He slid down from the gurney, *Yes ma'am*, and took out the pack, tapping it at the bottom.

As Al offered her the cigarette, a Secret Service agent appeared from nowhere and knocked the pack from his hand, breathing quickly, with wide terror eyes. He was about Al's age. Jittery. He looked at Al like he didn't know what was supposed to happen next.

The pack sat on the tile. All three stared at it.

Finally, the agent picked it up, squinted his eyes for an inspection, and then offered it to Mrs. Kennedy. After she took a single cigarette, the agent returned the pack. A pantomime act. All done without words.

Leaning into the match, her face temporarily disappeared. Just an orange light. She held the cigarette to her mouth without inhaling, and then knocked a bit of ash to the floor.

Maybe this was the proper time to say something. But the words were still way beyond him.

She took a long drag, holding the smoke in for an extra beat and then blowing it upward in a veil. "Where are you from?" she asked, before it cleared.

Al hoped she didn't mean *Where do you work*. He could probably get away with just saying "ambulance driver," but he didn't want to get into anything about caskets. Especially not when the doctors were only several feet away, trying to keep the holes in her husband's body from leaking. "I'm from Dallas, ma'am," Al stammered. "I live here in Dallas." Was someone else talking for him?

She asked what it was like, living in Texas, and he told her it was fine. That Texas was what he knew. Kind of hot but you get used to it. She looked right at him, her eyes sincere and soft, as though she felt responsible for making *him* feel comfortable.

They didn't talk much after that. They smoked quietly together, like strangers at a bar with an unspoken understanding. And they shared coffee brought by a candy striper who nearly had the stripes scared off her pinafore when the Secret Service pounced from all directions at her silver serving tray. And though Al and Mrs. Kennedy hardly spoke a word, there was a sense that their unlikely pairing was all they had to rely on. Together they sat in the shared silence, blocking out the chaos around them, until around one o'clock, when Dr. Kemp Clark, Agent Kellerman, and Ken O'Donnell said they needed to talk with Mrs. Kennedy. In private.

Inside the trauma room, Al tried to swallow, but he had no breath. The overhead lights burned, and the smell was antiseptic. Peanuts, Nurse Nelson, and Al waited for a priest, which seemed to take forever. It wasn't the sight of President Kennedy's body that threw him—he'd handled many bodies in his day, and although the president's head was wrapped with towels so thick that only a patch of brown blood had soaked through, it wasn't nearly as bad as some of the manglings he'd had to work with. Nor was it the cocktail of chaos and quiet, the failed-savior faces of the doctors, or the nurses' continuous swallowing to hold back tears. It was seeing Mrs. Kennedy not more than two feet away, looking at her husband. She'd come into the room several times, unsure of what to do, as though she'd been working herself up to something. Each time she stood a little closer to her husband's body. A strange blend of lightness and weight. Frail and broken, but still larger than life. Beautifully dressed. Her hair done. Too perfect for a moment like this.

This time Mrs. Kennedy looked as though she had a sense of purpose. She stood still, only her back rising in shallow breaths.

Reaching out to the trauma table where her husband lay, Mrs. Kennedy pulled the sheet back to his waist.

She slipped off her wedding ring, tucking it into her left palm. Then she pulled at his left hand, folded across his bare chest. His fingers dangled stiffly as the arm lifted. Mrs. Kennedy tried to slide her ring onto his finger. Al just watched her. The ring was half the size of the president's finger; still, she twisted it with delicate but violent determination. Without speaking, Al grabbed a tube of K-Y Jelly from the sink counter. He reached around her and dabbed a few drops onto the president's finger. His hand touched her sleeve. Mrs. Kennedy swiveled the ring, able to work it down a little. In tandem, Al squirted on a little more jelly. Her hand grazed his as she pushed with a little more force, managing to work the ring to the midknuckle. Mrs. Kennedy didn't look up, neither did Al. For a moment, in the silence of that room, they might have been the only two people breathing.

Al wheeled the casket out of the room along with the doctors, presidential staff, and agents—some helping, some in tow. Waiting for the priest, there had been a strange sense of hope. The plausibility of miracles. The potential for gigantic misunderstandings. But once Father Huber arrived to give conditional rites, it was as though all the lights dimmed, and the forms behind the shadows were finally revealed.

Al tried to stare straight ahead, moving the president down the corridor with one hand on the gurney and the other on top of the casket. The agents formed a V to unclog the pathway, and the procession was pure silence. Just wheels squeaking across the linoleum.

Mrs. Kennedy was opposite Al, her head bowed, gliding as if she too were rolling. When he and Peanuts had laid President Kennedy in the casket, Mrs. Kennedy was backed up against a wall. Never taking her eyes off her husband. She had gasped when the lid snapped shut. The only sound she'd made. Now her hand was holding on to the casket.

Father Huber kept pace, saying prayers and sprinkling holy water. Occasional drops hit Al's hand. One hit his cheek. Most just streaked down the bronze.

Near the exit, the procession stopped, as though it had run into a wall. A middle-aged man in a tweed sport coat pressed himself against the head of the casket. "I'm sorry, gentlemen," he said. He sounded both proud and scared. "But I can't allow the body to go any farther."

Agent Kellerman walked up to him. Wasting no time. Al was sick with anticipation. As if today were layer upon layer of people's bad dreams. "This is the President of the United States," Kellerman said, drumming his index finger against his thumb. "You need to move out of the way, mister."

"Doctor." The man in the tweed sport coat emphasized his title. "Dr. Earl Rose, chief of forensics." He drew in a breath, as though he were about to deliver a prepared speech. "This body cannot be removed until an autopsy and inquest are completed. There has been a murder committed here in Dallas, and Texas law states that any victim of murder has to have a proper autopsy before the body is removed. This is a Texas criminal investigation now."

Although their tones were hushed, Al could hear every word. Mrs. Kennedy, standing beside him, must have heard also. She kept her head bowed. Al inched his hand a little closer toward hers.

Kellerman asserted that as chief of the president's detail, he was going to politely ask the doctor to remove himself at once. This wasn't some gangland murder. This was the President of the United States, and Mrs. Kennedy would be with the body at every moment, so, please. Kellerman barked, growled, and tried to muscle the casket forward.

Rose held his grip. "Don't you understand?" he said, trying to keep his voice below a holler. "You have to maintain the chain of evidence. We have laws to uphold. You just don't understand." His lips trembled.

Father Huber continued to pray and to sprinkle holy water.

"Damn it," Kellerman said. "Just move the hell out of our way."

Another agent knocked Rose's hand off the casket and pushed him aside while Rose continued to insist that the autopsy had to be done in Dallas, muttering comments about notating every detail for his official report and wanting everybody's name, grousing that this stunk of something. He stopped talking when Mrs. Kennedy passed. Al didn't think the doctor looked ashamed. Just respectful.

Under the fluorescents, Al saw his palm prints on the bronze.

As they went through the glass doors, Al managed to pull his sleeve down around his hand. He moved up to the front and started polishing the top of the casket. Short, circular movements. Starting near the head, and then, in slow, concentric patterns, working his way out wider and wider.

— — — — —

The O'Neal Funeral Home was not compensated for the casket until 1965. It took two years of wrangling. On January 7, 1964, Vernon O'Neal submitted an invoice for $3,995 to the financial management division of the U.S. General Services Administration, director of data and financial management. On the invoice, he merely wrote, "Solid double wall Bronze Casket and all services rendered at Dallas, Texas." He shouldn't have been surprised when the bill was returned, directing him to itemize his services. Each item would need to be evaluated individually, with the payment to be determined. It would be given prompt attention, he was told.

One month later, O'Neal revised the invoice to $3,495 and submitted it to the GSA's Region 7 office, writing on the bill that the $500 reduction indicated, "Less charges which includes embalming, use of chapel, automotive equipment, professional services, etc." When he handed over the bill, O'Neal declared that that was all the itemizing he was doing. This was standard practice, and he was done.

In conjunction with the Kennedy family, the GSA officials concluded that the cost was too high. They didn't necessarily dispute the price of the casket, but felt that the value of the "services" had been overestimated.

In April of the same year, Vernon O'Neal flew to Washington, D.C., to reclaim his casket. He went to Gawler's Sons, the funeral home that had prepared the president's body for rest in his permanent casket. Vernon O'Neal wanted the bronze casket he'd provided. He was prepared to take it back to Dallas and display it in his showroom. Gawler's Sons sent him to the government officials. More than one person told him this would not be possible. *Then pay me,* he said. *Give us an itemized bill that is fair and honest,* they replied.

It will be given prompt attention, he was told.

— — — — —

Out on the ambulance dock, Mrs. Kennedy insisted on riding with the casket. Al tried explaining to the Secret Service that it wasn't safe. He'd have to keep the rollers down in the hearse and angle the casket in sideways, meaning that it couldn't hook on to the peg that was there to keep it from moving and shifting. If she sat in the jump seat, a quick turn could cause the casket to smash her. But the Secret Service men weren't listening. She could ride back there if she wanted to.

Al and Peanuts loaded the casket into the back of the hearse, rocking and angling it to make it fit. Mrs. Kennedy stood to the side. He was aware of how she watched every move. It should've made him nervous, but her presence gave Al comfort. He opened the door for her and reached down to lift the jump seat, which was flattened on the floor. Seating her there was a bad idea, but it was out of his hands now. Al nodded to Mrs. Kennedy to let her know it was ready. She looked in and then froze in place, looking uncertain of how she'd get down into the well. Taking her elbow, Al gently guided her. Then the moment changed with a flash of light, and the sun burnt straight into his eyes, and it was hard to breathe, and Al realized he was pinned against the car by Secret Service men, his arm pulled behind his back.

Mrs. Kennedy stopped. She glared at them. Without raising her voice above a whisper, she delivered a censure that would keep Al going for the rest of his life: "Leave that young man alone. That's the only gentleman I've met since I've been here."

It would be a quick ride up Harry Hines. Al knew he could get them to Love Field in a matter of minutes. But he'd need to drive slowly, to ensure Mrs. Kennedy's safety in back. O'Neal took one last drag off his Kool and then walked up to Kellerman in his bowlegged confidence, telling him they'd meet the agents at the tarmac. There was no time to see O'Neal's expression change. Before he was even done talking, three agents jumped into the back of the hearse, two more in front. Kellerman ignored O'Neal, and slid into the driver's seat. Police cleared the way. Bystanders leaned in. Tears and pale faces. Almost prostrate against the car. When finally there was an opening in the crowd, Kellerman gunned the car, taking it out of sight.

O'Neal looked at Al, and then back at his disappearing car. "Goddamn," he said. "Why, all those sons of bitches done stole my hearse."

Al nodded, watching the top of Mrs. Kennedy's head fade away, hoping those sons of bitches didn't take a curve too sudden.

— — — — —

Sometime during the four hours it took to autopsy President Kennedy's body at Bethesda Naval Hospital, a new casket was picked out for him. Larry O'Brien, who later went on to be commissioner of the National Basketball Association, had been waiting with Kenny O'Donnell and Dave Powers when he noticed that the handles on the bronze casket were bent. He turned to his colleagues and said, "God, we have to get a new casket." Moments later they were in a car, heading to Gawler's Sons on Wisconsin Avenue. They took an elevator up to the showroom, repeating over and over that they wanted to see the "middle-priced" caskets. Not the low end. And not the high. Only the "middle-priced" caskets. They selected a mahogany model, and had it and the bill dispatched to the hospital.

Gawler's Sons' bill itemized everything. They were used to working with the government. *Embalming. Shaving, dressing, and casketing the body. Services of funeral director and staff at the church and cemetery. Necessary Equipment. Wilbert Triune Vault. Solid mahogany casket, as selected. Total Services and merchandise: $3,160.* They were paid immediately.

Years later Larry O'Brien was asked why they insisted on a middle-priced casket. "I think what you were grasping for in your mind was he was one of the people," O'Brien said. "He was sort of typical of America, an average American."

— — — — —

Peanuts and Al went out to eat at the waffle shop across the street from the O'Neal Funeral Home. It was eight o'clock, and by then nothing else was open. They hadn't known what to do for the rest of the day, so they kept themselves busy doing lots of little somethings. They hadn't spoken much. In fact, they'd barely even looked at each other most of the afternoon. They walked against the traffic light to the waffle shop and took their usual seats. They didn't bother to look at the menu. Al told the waitress that he'd have a grilled cheese and a malt, and Peanuts looked up at her and said, "Make that two." She looked at both of them kind of sad, and then she swallowed a lump so big anybody could've seen it and turned away.

The food came quickly. Whereas they normally would have devoured it after a long day, both Peanuts and Al just stared at their plates now. The waitress sat on a stool at the end of the counter. She kept counting her checks over and over, in between fiddling with her nylons.

Al looked at Peanuts. Neither one had touched his dinner. "Let's go," he said. "I don't have much of an appetite."

It was a silent walk back to O'Neal's. Al was afraid to talk, knowing the way things can build and build inside a person. He didn't know what he might say or how he might say it.

Once inside the funeral home, he walked straight back into the casket room, closed the door, and cried like he'd never cried before. Crying for all the strength he'd had to have that day. Crying for Mrs. Kennedy. And crying for the fact that he knew tomorrow would be coming no matter what, and he'd wake up again in his same bed, wondering if he'd done enough to make yesterday better.

Al Rike wanted to hang up the phone while he was talking with his sister Carolyn. Once word got out that he'd actually been in the trauma room, she was one of many callers. Al hadn't talked with any of the others, explaining he'd need to call back later, but he felt obligated not to brush Carolyn off as quickly. She had started the conversation saying, "Well?" And he said, "Well, what?" And she said, "You sure as heck know, 'Well, what?'"

He was forthcoming with a little information, at least, he thought, enough to satisfy her. She gasped when he confirmed that he'd been in the room with Mrs. Kennedy, and then there was a pause that sounded as if Carolyn might be crying. After regaining her composure, Carolyn started in with the questions. She wanted to know everything about the first lady, every detail and smell in the room.

Al stopped listening. And then he told her he didn't feel like talking about it right now.

She said, "You going to keep something like that to yourself? You need to share the information."

He bit down on the underside of his lip, trying to will an end to the conversation without her feeling offended. The afternoon was just so deep inside him that he didn't know how to tell it without a common language that would make it anybody's story. Even the little bits that he had said about Mrs. Kennedy felt detached already—just lifeless descriptions.

It was too soon to know if there would come a time when he'd talk nonstop about it. In fact, would there be a point when that was *all* he talked about? An hour or so in Parkland Memorial Hospital could define him, a calling card for the rest of his life. And as he would tell the story over the years, details might come and go. The experience may be refined. Sometimes he might be alone in the hospital room beside Mrs. Kennedy, other times he'd see her coming in and out of the room twice. Sometimes she dropped ashes, other times she didn't. Sometimes Peanuts had more to say, sometimes he was barely there. Sometimes the argument over the body might have taken place in the hallway or the nurses' station, sometimes in the doorway. Sometimes the ring slid onto the knuckle, sometimes it just stopped short. Sometimes Al's arm was pinned. Sometimes the sun was not so bright. Sometimes she scared him, sometimes she comforted him. And sometimes the whole day was what drove Al to become a police officer.

Sometimes. Sometimes. Sometimes.

All these bits and pieces might collaborate, turning into a story that will be told so many times that it ends up true.

But at that moment, Al wanted to be selfish. Bury it inside. His, alone.

— — — — —

Until February of 1966, the bronze casket remained in storage in the National Archives in College Park, Maryland. It seems as though it was Bobby Kennedy's idea to get rid of it, arguing that it belonged to his family and they could do with it what they pleased. Bobby is quoted in a phone conversation as saying, "What I would like to have done is take it to sea." One can imagine that Vernon O'Neal's initial persistence to take back the casket and display it in his Dallas mortuary must have spurred on the family's need to destroy it. That thought had to be horrifying.

The main concern expressed to Bobby was that his plan might be perceived as destroying evidence, and that in addition to the public perception, there could also be a legal issue. Lawson Knott, the administrator at the General Services Administration office, told Bobby that he needed authorization from the Department of Justice. On February 11, 1966, Nicholas Katzenbach, Bobby's former deputy attorney general, who had now assumed the role of attorney general, wrote to Knott, explaining that he saw no possible evidentiary value to the casket. He expressed concern about its potential for public display, terming that notion "extremely offensive and contrary to public policy." And, on a practical matter, he noted that it was clear that the casket could never be used for burial purposes.

The casket was weighted with two hundred and forty pounds' worth of sandbags and loaded onto a C-130 at Andrews Air Force base. It was February 16. 8:38 AM. The plane headed out over the Atlantic near Delaware, away from all traffic and commercial activities. At ten o'clock the casket was shoved out the tail hatch, guided down by parachutes. It landed softly, with only a trace of impact. It left no bubbles as it sank into the sea.

MRS. KENNEDY
IS ORGANIZING HERSELF

IT'S LIKE IT IS WITH BIRDS. They hide their wounds and diseases. Instinctively they know they are prey, and any sign of weakness puts them at mortal risk. So by daylight the sick bird stands proud and tall, singing to the morning. And it is a song of longing, one of beauty and one of grace. The kind of song that causes all to take notice. But at night that bird closes her eyes, afraid she won't wake up to see the next day. Afraid her song already will be forgotten.

Jackie sits on a plane, or is it in the emergency room—no, it must be a plane. It must be Air Force One. Already she has spent too much time in hospitals. Grief has become a part of her. Like a growth inside.

The plane idles on the tarmac at Love Field, shaking and rattling, the smell of fumes leaking through the vents. And though she sits in a quiet space, there is a constant bustle around her. She can hear the reporters moving through the cabin, balancing reverence and duty. The press is being hastily arranged: Johnson can't wait; his political instinct is too developed. Almost freakish. Despite the staging, they give her space. The bedroom, all to herself. Nobody knows what to do. Someone had asked if she wanted company, and she'd nodded her head. They took that as a no. They're trying to be respectful, she supposes.

The plane jolts again, as though a large cache of luggage is being loaded. She figures it is her husband. She feels for her wedding ring before remembering how she placed it on his finger once the surgeons had given up. It's only been an hour and twenty minutes, but it feels like a lifetime ago. It seems impossible that he is lying in a casket. It also seems impossible that he was sitting next to her when the day started. Already he is being reduced to a series of still memories. Even his blood on her dress seems like an old stain or part of the pattern.

But she waits. Rubbing her hands together, sometimes too sweaty, sometimes not sweaty enough, made emptier by the absence of her ring. In her arm is a pain from the needle's stick. It would calm her down, the doctor said. But she wanted more than calm. *Don't you have something that can make it all go away? Something that will reverse time?* She didn't say that. She should have.

Jackie waits in the bedroom. She is only waiting because she has been told to wait. Always the good girl. The one who waits.

Sophisticated.
Charming.
Graceful.
Demure.
She used to be known by adjectives. Now she is just an object. There are no modifiers to describe her.

Kenny O'Donnell knocks on the door. He peers in without opening it all the way. Although his hair is parted evenly with the combed streaks still kempt, his face looks tired, drawn, and pale, like someone who knows 4 AM. He doesn't appear confident, nor does he seem weak. He says her name once. His eyes keep to the floor. "Mrs. Kennedy," he says again. Even from where she sits, she can smell the tobacco on his breath.

She isn't ignoring him. It's just that she has forgotten how to speak. The same way one momentarily forgets how to tie her shoes, or spell the simplest of words, or her first pet's name. If she could speak, she would tell him it's okay to look her in the eye.

"They'll be swearing in the new president momentarily," he says. "He requests that you be there. Johnson wants you by his side."

If she could speak, she would tell him no. That she cannot imagine anything more humiliating and distasteful. But she can't speak. All she can do is shake her head.

"*For the good of the country*, Johnson is saying." O'Donnell looks at the wall, almost ashamed at the words coming out of his mouth. He clearly has been sent to convince her. That's not surprising, though. The industry of politics is about persuasion, not conviction. He starts to speak again, but then stops. "Ten minutes," he says, looking at his watch. "Ten minutes until the swearing in."   •

She continues to shake her head.

"Mrs. Kennedy, I know this is . . . But the eyes of the world *are* watching. The public needs to know that we will be okay."

"Okay?" She is not sure if she said that or just thought it. But she sees O'Donnell swallow, the lump in his throat grown cancerously, while a bead of sweat forms just above his eyebrows. He licks his lips and then smacks them, as though he intended to say something. But there is just a helpless breath.

Part of her would really like to believe that this will all be over in ten minutes. That they'll be okay. But Jack's blood is still on her dress. His hair still on the pillow. Her lipstick still on what is left of his cheek. Maybe in politics the story line can shift that quickly, but this is her life, and she can't just swear in somebody new to put things back to normal. At this point, she doesn't even believe in *normal*. Nothing will heal this. The doctors can try to pump her full of Vistaril and other drugs to dull her nerves, but there isn't a medication invented yet that can reach that place inside her that will not stop screaming, the one that even God can't touch.

"Mrs. Kennedy, it is important that you . . ."

"You really think . . . ?"

"I do."

She drops her face into her palms. There is no way. She cannot imagine posing with Johnson. Being before cameras. She jerks up suddenly, unsure of whose hands are touching her face. Feeling the confidence of words in her throat. "Tell him I'm sorry, Kenny. Tell him I can't. Whatever you need to say."

"I wish you would reconsider, Mrs. Kennedy. The country is looking to you for hope, Mrs. Kennedy. They're not looking to Johnson. They're looking to you."

She wishes she could believe him. But he seems too convinced, as though his loyalty has been questioned at the policy table. "And for whom are you speaking?" she asks.

This startles O'Donnell. He backs out of the doorway and then steps forward again. Voices rustle. A woman's voice, followed by a man's, a long, unfamiliar drawl that seems too jovial for the moment. And then she hears laughing. *Laughing?* Finally, there is a hush when footsteps rock the plane. Heavy and languid.

"Is he on board?" she asks.

"Judge Hughes is getting ready to administer the oath. Mrs. Johnson is also here."

"They fly on Air Force Two."

"He is practically president now, Mrs. Kennedy."

"But they fly on Air Force Two."

O'Donnell steps all the way into her quarters. He shuts the door behind him. "Jackie," he says, moving closer to her. "You know I . . ."

"No." She needs to cry, but they've got her so doped that it has dried her out.

"If Johnson had just done his job," O'Donnell says, "just kept control of Texas like he was supposed to, then . . . If he had just done what he was supposed to do."

"Worthless," she says. A simple, disdainful word. The perfect word for how she felt about having to take this trip. And Jack's aides all knew it, mumbling and groaning at taking a fund-raising trip to mend the fractures between Texas Democrats. Senator Yarborough and Governor Connally had been sniping, and Johnson, supposed to be the peacemaker, jumped right into it with Yarborough. Sniped at each other all through breakfast, and, like the parent of two petulant children, Jack insisted Yarborough and Johnson ride together in the motorcade. Smile and learn to get along. That's what the whole trip was for. What it's all ended up for. *Worthless.* She says it one more time, feeling that little bit of a scream work its way through her numbed body.

"Nevertheless, you're going to have be there, Jackie. I don't see any way . . ."

"Tell him no."

"I'll tell him you may not be up for it. That you are considering."

"Whom do you work for now, Kenny?"

"I don't like his people any more than Jack does."

"Jack's dead, Kenny."

"I'm sorry."

She pauses and considers how little control she has; has it been lost that easily? *Worthless*, she thinks.

"I'll tell him you need more time."

By August of 1963 it is hard to argue that the value of a human life has not diminished. The population of the world has grown five times in the past hundred years. In this year alone the world seems content to take without conscience or measure. Over one hundred killed in Vietnam. More than four thousand killed between the earthquakes and the landslides. Yugoslavia. Liberia. Chad. Japan. Italy. Birmingham. The innocent die as quickly as they wake up.

On August 7, life does matter. Jackie is in labor, and in the back of the ambulance she heaves with each contraction. Her face is red, and she can't make a fist because her hands are too weak and too wet. Although she is ready for this to end, for a moment she thinks she needs to keep the baby inside, protect him just a little bit longer from the world he is about to enter. And she really wishes she had the physical ability to do that, but the boy is stubborn, and too eager to submit.

He is born Patrick Bouvier Kennedy, named in honor of his two grandfathers. As though his first inhalation sucks in the sins of his heritage, Patrick is found to have a lung disease and is pronounced dead two days later.

Despite the state of the world, she thinks, the value of his life will not be diminished. That will be validated when the world mourns with her. But they'll mourn a little more softly. These days there is not enough to go around.

Jackie can't even think about it. Is Kenny O'Donnell playing her? Maybe he is just another political hack who holds allegiances only as long as they are breathing. He had palled around with the Kennedy boys as far back as Harvard, been working with Jack since the Senate campaign, but now he seems too resolute. He was just one car back in the motorcade. Surely he must have seen the explosion of blood. Seen the springs and coils burst out of the body machine. Smelled the almost-instant rot of exposed brain the way she did. In this room, it feels as if she is the only one who cares. The only one who recognizes the tragedy.

Jackie already knows that she will hate herself for thinking that about Kenny. But it doesn't change the moment. It doesn't make it any more certain that when he knocks again, she will square her shoulders as best she can and rise to welcome him into the room before allowing him to escort her to the cabin to stand beside Johnson, who is likely to rush the oath with the same purpose in which he pushed for this trip, before he scurries off to have the furniture moved, the rocking chair taken out, creepy bull's horns and dried-up cow skulls brought in, where he'll tell those long, ginned-up, boring stories that are such contrivances that only he believes, all with his crass smile and conspiring smirk, a little too comfortable in the Oval Office, already forgetting how he got there. That's what standing next to him will bring. What her presence will validate.

She can't give in. She needs to hold on to Jack a little longer.

However, their skills of persuasion are far greater than her resolve—especially in this condition. Maybe if Bobby were here. Maybe if Jack weren't lying in a casket in the back of the plane.

She knows they'll wear her down. Eventually. They always do. Always do.

There is a knock on the door again, short little knuckled raps, followed by O'Donnell's voice saying "Mrs. Kennedy. Mrs. Kennedy."

This time she does not invite him in. Instead she says, "No," and she can visualize the two-letter word floating across the room and quietly yet firmly bolting the door shut.

He knocks again. This time with a bit more urgency. "Mrs. Kennedy." He speaks as though someone is monitoring him. "Mrs. Kennedy."

It is not silence on her part, it is a lack of reply. The noise is loud and clear. Behind the door a woman talks to Kenny, rushing through jargon and logistics. But then the woman's voice lowers, and all Jackie can make out is *first lady*. Once with a question mark, the next followed by an exclamation point.

It is a title she had tried to resist. She didn't want to fit into someone else's coat. But now the thought of not having it—of not being *first lady*—seems worse. She had it thrust upon her, and now it's been stripped away just as easily. The Johnson people will minimize her as quickly as possible. They will want her to disappear. Vanish like breath on a chilled morning.

It is a terrible existence to be constantly afraid of losing it all.

Jackie still keeps dresses on consignment in Cambridge, collecting the money and laundering it away just in case. They are not the premier gowns from the magazine spreads and statehouse dinners; instead, she sells the dresses that are gifts, the comps that come in weekly, occasionally worn to a luncheon, though rarely unfolded from the box. All the labels are recognizable, the quality exquisite. It's not a huge take, but every bit helps her to feel a little more secure.

Perhaps when your father leaves you at ten nothing ever seems sure. The first loose pebble in the landslide? Or another way of looking at it: the gift that allows you to see into your future, giving you ample time to prepare for what lies ahead.

In the mirror her hair looks dry and dirty, giving Jackie the pale dullness of the unwashed. "Go away," she yells at the door. "Go away." But there isn't a sound. Has she lost her ability to speak? Screaming and screaming when nobody hears is not necessarily a sign of craziness—more likely, it's that nobody cares what you have to say.

And it is unfair, this idea of mechanics and engineering, where a metal hammer no larger than her little finger can rocket a teeny fragment into a skull in only seconds, boring in just deep enough to drain out all the life. Nothing of consequence should be able to change that quickly. And she thinks of her children, of how she will even begin to explain to them what this all means. They haven't lived in the world of risk. They are too young to know the unsteadiness of the ground beneath them.

O'Donnell finally walks into the room without formality. He swings the door closed but it doesn't catch all the way. It bounces and settles, leaving just a sliver of light. The noises of the outside world seep through. Voices rising. Cameras loading. Papers shuffling. Adrenaline and anxiety set loose. Jackie knows the soundtrack.

"Only for my children," she says before O'Donnell can speak. "I will only do it for my children. And I am not changing my dress. No pageants."

O'Donnell nods his head, biting his bottom lip. "Okay," he says. "Okay." His index finger presses into his cheek. If she didn't know better, she would think all this bored him.

"No pageants. It's not for him. Not for Johnson."

"Okay."

"I want you to tell his people that. In fact, I want you to tell Johnson himself that I am only coming out for my children. To let them know that their father can't leave that easily. I just can't validate worthlessness. I need that to be clear. Are you going to tell him, Kenny? Are you going to make that clear to Johnson?"

O'Donnell continues to nod his head. What else can he do? He has no choice but to forgive her demands and reasoning. Jackie can see her reflection in his eyes, and it is not just a literal refraction, but the way his brain is seeing her. It causes her to pause. In the last hour and a half she hasn't stopped to consider anything. She is a pure form of trauma.

She stands up, weightless, already floating on her feet.

Looking in all directions, she tries to catalog and inventory everything around her, from the rumpled dent in the bed to the red finger marks on O'Donnell's face to the smell in the room, which still smells of last night, of normal. It is important to remember. Because despite her justifications and demands about the swearing-in, this new administration is about to create its own vision of history. O'Donnell probably won't say anything to Johnson, and even if he does, it won't be heard. She will be posed beside the incoming president, arranged like a decorative stem to look as if she is giving him her full support and trust. The photographs will preserve that moment until, like the rest of the world, she will have to maintain vigilance not to believe their version, too.

But for now she will try.

Her legacy will still matter. The memories will not be whitewashed and then covered with a fresh coat. At least not yet. Not here on a plane, with her husband's freshly murdered body lying in cargo, on a tarmac in Dallas, at an airport called Love Field, proving that the world does not need poets, it does a fine job in creating its own sense of irony.

ZAPRUDER'S VIEWFINDER

The Bell & Howell 414 DP Discovery Series Movie Camera.

Thoroughly reading the user's manual will ensure that the camera captures what it sees in the most accurate way.

Start with the basics:
> » How to operate the Start button (Page 7)
> » Loading the film (Page 2)
> » The Zoomatic lens (Pages 5, 6, 10)
> » Electric Eye operation (Page 8)
> » Built-in filters (Page 4)
> » Zoomatic Viewfinder (Page 5)

And make sure to read the tips:
> » "Don't zoom too much. Like any good technique, it will be most effective when used sparingly." (Page 11)

» "If your fingers block the Electric Eye when you shoot, your camera will not 'see' things in their proper light. Don't confuse the camera. Make sure it sees everything." (Page 12)

» "Try to plan your movies so that they'll tell a story with continuity and interest . . . Once you're familiar with the Electric Eye camera you can take thrilling automatic movies you'll always be proud to show." (Page 9)

It's all about resisting the temptation to control the camera. To think it can see what you see. Because that's where the whole process can falter. Forgetting that the camera acts as its own witness.

The Interview.

About an hour and a half after the shooting, Abe Zapruder is in the studios of WFAA-TV. He is seated at a desk next to Jay Watson, the station's program director, who is not used to being in front of the camera. Watson smokes furiously, his attention scattered, taking phone calls on the air while simultaneously introducing his guest. There's barely an inch between them. Initially Abe looks comfortable in his jacket and bow tie, as though he's hosting his own television show. Still, he swivels as he talks. It's in his eyes. Where the composure starts to wilt.

Watson asks, "Would you tell us your story, please, sir?" and Abe starts at a half hour before the shooting. Talks about finding the spot. Clears his throat. And he hears the shot. Models how Kennedy slumped. In describing the next gunshot (*I couldn't say if it was one or two*), he says he saw Kennedy's "head practically open up, all blood and everything, and I kept on shooting. That's about all, I'm just sick, I can't . . ." Here you sense him breaking, but still there is an incompleteness to it all. There clearly is shock. Anguish. But it is deeper than that. As though part of his memory is in that camera.

Maybe sensing this, Watson reminds Abe that they do have the movie camera in the studio, and "We'll try to get that processed and have it as soon as possible." Then the station cuts to coverage of the hearse leaving Parkland Memorial Hospital. This is the collective memory. The real-time experience. And in the interview, you can almost see Abe contemplate trying to hang on to his memories. Somehow knowing that once the film is developed, his memory will become part of the collective. A commonplace experience. Maybe that's why he ends the interview the way he does. Brings it back to the first blast, when he still thought it was a joke, like when you "hear a shot and somebody grabs their stomach." Maybe that's all he has left. Something no film footage will co-opt. That little bit of shame is all his.

Background.

Just forty years ago in the Ukraine, Abraham Zapruder was watching his neighbors and fellow Jews being terrorized and slaughtered during the Russian civil war. The Zapruder family escaped because the fight would be futile; an escape that he remembers as both cowardly and brave. They emigrated from Kovel to Brooklyn when he was fifteen. At thirty-six, Abe left Brooklyn for Dallas to found his own dress-manufacturing business, two floors' worth. Abe is a man who recognizes hope and opportunity when he sees it. He knows it can come in all sorts of disguises. How the unexpected moments can be the ones that most inspire you.

On Elm.

Kennedy was riding on his side of the street. Leaning forward. Smiling. Waving. For just one second, Abe wanted to lower the camera and see the president with his own eyes. But he was determined to capture Kennedy. He was glad he'd brought the camera. He had not intended to. It would only get in the way of seeing the president. That's what he'd told Lillian, his secretary at Jennifer Juniors. The reason he gave her. He wanted to see Kennedy for himself. Not just steady a camera that was doing the actual seeing. Lillian convinced him otherwise. Told him he had time to go home to get the camera. Twenty minutes round trip, tops. Seven miles each way. She told him he must have been a mind reader to open his dress business on Elm Street. *Front row seats for the Kennedys, Mr. Z. Make use of it.* He'll be glad to have this memory. Go on, Lillian kept at him. She got his other receptionist, Marilyn, in on it. *Really, Mr. Z,* they went on.

He thought about traffic. About parking. How with the expected mob coming downtown, twenty minutes could turn into hours. But it was just a little past eight. He supposed he had time, even in the worst-case scenario. Plus it would be something to have a movie of Kennedy. *Think about your grandchildren, Mr. Z. It's the Kennedys, Mr. Z. Isn't this just the thing you bought the camera for?* And they started to get to him, Lillian and Marilyn. This would be the story to tell his future generations. Not of pogroms or daring yet ambivalent escapes. Rather, of when he was just feet away from John F. Kennedy.

The day had started rainy and hazy, lighting that would complicate any filming. If it did start to pour, would he switch to the Haze Filter, or just leave the Type A all the way out? It wouldn't make for much of a movie, having to film through all the umbrellas, not to mention that the president likely would be covered up in his car, just waving through the window. But those concerns were soon lost. The sun came out, and as quickly the day turned more springlike. *The Kennedys bring sunshine wherever they go,* one of the office gals said. Abe smiled. He was not one for platitudes. But he did believe it.

Rushing out of the Dal-Tex Building at 501 Elm Street, Abe and Marilyn crossed the street, sidestepping their way through the School Book Depository employees that had crowded the sidewalk. He moved quickly. Glancing back at the route. Seeing it as though he were the camera lens. Looking for the right perspective. The best angle. With Marilyn still trailing he continued down Elm, toward the underpass. He checked his watch. Looked back up the street. Some other employees from Jennifer Juniors had caught up with them. But he didn't talk to them. Just kept moving. Getting closer to the underpass.

Finally he found a big concrete square, nearly four feet high. He lassoed the camera to his wrist as he climbed up. The sun was over his shoulder for ideal lighting. He checked his watch again. According to the published schedule, there were at least ten minutes to spare before the motorcade was due to pass through. He took a long breath and wiped the sweat off his forehead.

He pointed the camera at his employees, reviewing the user's manual in his head. They looked at him. Smiled. One shaded her face, turning her back to him. *I'm just testing,* he said. *Running a few frames to make sure she's working okay.* He zoomed in on them. Standing on the grass. A marble slab in the background. He pushed the Start button. Listened for the clicking. Moved the zoom in, moved the zoom out. He called to Marilyn once he stopped. *Can you stand behind me?* he asked. *I don't know why, but this telephoto lens spins my head a bit. Makes me dizzy. If you can just stand behind me. Maybe hold my coattail to keep me balanced.* And together they stood there. Looking up Elm toward Houston. Waiting for the limousine to make the turn.

The next thing he knew he was yelling out, *They killed him. They killed him.* Running up the grassy knoll. Toward the pergola. *They killed him. They killed him.* His body screamed. His mind couldn't make sense. A moment ago Kennedy had been clowning around. And now. *They killed him.* He didn't even know how he got off the abutment. He was ghostlike. Walking through walls. Through people. Calling out, chanting, *They killed him. They killed him.*

What's happening? people asked him. *What's happening?*

They killed him. And each time he said it, it seemed another person wilted and fell away.

The camera still hung from his wrist. It banged against his thigh. Hitting the same place over and over. Pummeling him black and blue.

At the Dal-Tex Building.

Abe slumps forward on his desk. The television news is playing. The movie camera sits on top of the filing cabinet. It's unfairly still.

Somewhere there is a breath in his chest.

Darwin Payne from the *Times Herald* is in his office. Sitting across from him, talking with his hands. Payne will help him get the film developed, he says. This movie is that important. But Abe can barely speak, other than to say he knows Kennedy is dead. He knows he's dead. The TV news anchors can say what they want. They can talk hopefully about wounds—even serious wounds—but Abe knows Kennedy is dead. He saw it through the viewfinder.

Finally he gathers the strength to brush Payne away, explaining that someone from *Life* contacted him first, and though he doesn't know what is what, he is a man of his word. As he closes the door behind Payne, Abe's not sure if the film is news, commerce, or evidence. At this point, it's physiology and technology. The rest of the people there witnessed the moment of the killing, and then that quickly it was gone. But Abe Zapruder has a record of what his eye saw. It's sitting on his file cabinet. Waiting to be processed. A visual replica of his memory. And, looking up at the camera again, he considers just popping open the door and exposing the film. A drastic surgical remedy.

Lillian walks in, saying something he can't hear. Something about government men. Waiting. She's walking with a transistor radio in her hand. It's static and chaos. She's crying, sniffling while she pats at her pockets for a tissue. She says the men are in the outer office, and then she reports that the radio just said the president is only wounded, to which Abe replies, *I know he's dead.* Lillian eyes the TV and then turns up the radio, trying to make out more announcements through the static.

Abe stands to greet the government men. For a moment disoriented. Confused between the noise outside the window and the sounds on the radio and the TV. He could close his window, but somehow it's reassuring, hearing the sirens, and hearing all those people still milling in the plaza. Hearing their moans and their cries. He is a little less alone.

A True Story.

The night of November 22, Abe had a nightmare that he was walking through Times Square. There he passed a barker standing in front of some unsavory movie house. The barker called out, "Hey folks, come on in and see the president killed on the big screen."

The Screening.

By 8 AM on November 23, Abe is showing the film to Secret Service agents. It's an empty room on one of his floors in the Dal-Tex Building. There are no windows. No screen. Only a couple of folding chairs and a card table set up in the middle to hold the projector. The overhead lights are off, just the projector's white light beaming a small but distinct square on the blank white wall.

The fan on the projector whirrs. Almost like a jet engine.

Abe stands beside it and asks, *Are you ready, gentlemen?*

Ready, Mr. Zapruder.

He fiddles with the knobs, trying to sharpen the focus on the edges of the blank picture. *Okay now,* he says. *So you are ready?*

They nod, looking impatient, checking their watches, and documenting the time on their notepads. Abe knows they're not really ready. He's seen the film. Seen how the mind plays funny tricks. Experienced how the first twenty seconds fill you with hope and excitement. And there is still the strange possibility that what you know is going to happen may not happen. Yet it does. You realize how vague hope really is.

Abe starts the film. The reels on the 8 mm projector click just off the beat. Turning round and round, repetitious. The makeshift screen has filled in with black. Scratches animate across the wall, lightning storms, off as quickly as they are on.

The agents shift. One taps his foot in time with the projector.

There is a long leader on the film, even after cutting off the home movies and the test footage he'd made before the parade. Then, abruptly, it starts. Here come the motorcycle cops twisting onto Elm, leading the motorcade. The sun is shining. Here comes the president.

Another True Story.

By 10:30 AM, after screening the twenty-four-second film over and over for various officials, Abe's office is flooded with reporters wanting access to the film. They're all speaking in controlled voices, guaranteeing something. But it is Richard Stolley, of *Life*, with whom he goes behind closed doors, despite the protests of the others. The garment industry is flat these days, he tells Stolley. Every year the business has been making its way closer to Mexico, and Dallas is as far south as Abe is willing to follow it. He worries for his family's future. Tells Stolley he wants them be secure. Still, he doesn't want to be part of exploiting the death of the president. The idea of being a profiteer seems shameful. Stolley reminds him that this is *Life*. Its reputation is its integrity. Stolley guarantees they'll be prudent in how they use the film. This is now part of the story of America, and, like it or not, Abe's film is one of the great documents of history. Through Stolley, *Life* pays $50,000 for the print rights. Two days later they pay an additional $100,000 for the original film, with payments to be disbursed annually at $25,000. Abe contributes the first payment to the Firemen's and Policemen's Benevolent Fund, with a donation suggestion for Mrs. J. D. Tippit. The balance goes to the Zapruder family's future.

Frame 313.

A movie camera connects a series of still pictures. A series of small moments. And each frame is assigned a number. In the case of his film, it is frame 313. That is the one where Kennedy's head bursts open. That sudden poof of red that is at once abstract and elliptical. Abe didn't need to lose the whole memory. Just frame 313. If it could have just been edited out. Then the worst part of the day only would've been his disappointment at Kennedy fooling around like he'd been shot after the loud pop, before the limousine disappeared beneath the underpass on the way to the Trade Mart.

The Testimony.

Giving up the film was supposed to relieve him. But there are some days that he swears he sees it in his head. Starting up with the scratchy leader, and then right to the motorcade. And then it's frame 313 over and over again. Backward and forward. Forward and backward. Until the motorcade disappears beneath the underpass. Some days it plays in his head several times. Sometimes only once or twice a week. But always the same pattern. Backward and forward. Forward and backward. And it occurs to him that his memory and the film are one and the same. That every time the film is studied in some Secret Service/FBI lab, or cut and spliced in New York at *Life*, it is somehow projecting through him.

By the time Abe is testifying for the Warren Commission, exactly eight months to the day have passed since he shot his film. Nearly down to the hour. He sits in the office of the U.S. attorney in Dallas, being questioned by Wesley Liebler, assistant counsel to the commission. Abe's nervous. In a way, he seems more shaken than he was in the hours following the assassination. He can't seem to get his words right. He knows what he's thinking, but it just won't translate. Maybe it's that the shock has worn off. Now it's an exposed wound.

Liebler is being gracious. Gentle. They start off with the background information. Abe tells him about not having the camera, going down to Elm Street, searching for the perfect spot until he found the concrete abutment. He's thorough. Comfortable with the logic of these details.

But shortly the motorcade is in front of him, and Liebler is asking more pointed questions. Frame by frame. Bullet by bullet. As he did on WFAA, Abe confesses he thought Kennedy was joking after the first shot. After eight months, he sounds a little more practiced. Still, the shame remains. He goes on to say, "I heard a second shot and I saw his head opened up and the blood and everything came out and I started—I can hardly talk about it . . ." and he falls forward, dropping his face into his hands, sobbing. He looks up once or twice. Takes in a breath, holding it, trying to compose himself, and then starts crying again.

"That's all right, Mr. Zapruder," Liebler says. "Would you like a drink of water? Why don't you step out of the room and have a drink of water?"

Abe doesn't move. He looks up, trying to regain his posture, but unable to look Liebler in the eyes. Fixing his stare on a knot in the paneling. "I'm sorry," he says. "I'm ashamed of myself really, but I couldn't help it . . . The whole thing that has been transpiring . . . It was very upsetting, and as you see, I got a little better all the time, and this came up again . . . And . . . It to me . . . Looked like a second shot."

They resume the deposition, continuing to take the day apart, frame by frame. He answers steadily. Keeps on track. He wants to be useful. And when Liebler is ready to wrap things up, he lets Abe know how helpful the film has been to the commission. Abe nods. "I'm only sorry I broke down," he says. "I didn't know I was going to do it."

Liebler thanks him. Repeats how helpful the film has been.

"Well, I'm ashamed of myself. I didn't know I was going to break down, and for a man to . . . but it was a tragic thing, and when you started asking me that, and I saw the thing all over again, and it was an awful thing . . . An awful thing."

And though they'll forever call him helpful for what he did, he wishes he'd had nothing to offer. That he'd left the camera at home. Wishes he'd never even cared about Kennedy. Because, in the end, all this has done is brought him shame. For thinking the wrong thing when the first bullet struck. For feeling as though he were selling out the horror for profit, scrambling to donate a chunk of the money as fast as it came in. For breaking down with childish tears. Imagine that. A Ukrainian Jew who escaped the pogroms and terrors of the Russian civil war, who came to America and built himself into a businessman, just to become someone who can't compose himself, all for what he saw through his viewfinder. At least he was able to provide for his family. For that he can feel no shame.

THE OATH OF OFFICE

Within Twenty-four Seconds.

Jack screamed out, and she fell forward, and it sounded like firecrackers, and Jackie's first thought had been *Why on earth would they be shooting off fireworks? That's a strange thing to be doing.* It was hard to see what was what. Jackie only looked up once, but when she did, she found herself on the back of the limo, and she doesn't know what she was thinking, only that she might have believed herself dead. That her soul was climbing out of her body.

Then she's huddled down in the backseat. Hunkering. Taking refuge. Clint Hill lying on top of them. Jack's foot sticking up out of the car. She's trying to tug it down. Hiding from where she thinks the shots are coming from.

People can say what they want about her class and her debutante poise, but once those shots were flying, she was all over him, willing to take the bullets. And Jackie knows she would have if they hadn't found Jack first.

Walking Spanish: Part One.

It's not a long walk through the airplane, from the bedchamber to the presidential suite. But it's long enough. She keeps her hands to her sides. No one seems to notice her. Not Kenny or Larry or Pam or Mac or anybody else from Jack's staff. They must be in the compartment already, waiting for the administration of the oath. It's taking her forever to walk the short distance, but she trusts she can. Her body is dulled, and her head just as dulled. But she can sense her mind working rapidly, processing and dismissing at equal rate. A paralyzing contradiction. Still, as she moves forward, closer and closer to the swearing-in, she is moving further away from what she knows. There's an expression she remembers from a novel or a movie. *Walking Spanish.* When a sailor is being dragged through a ship before being forced to walk the plank. *Walking Spanish.*

Within Twenty-eight Seconds: Part One.

Lyndon's holding her hands. His are big like clown gloves, and they cover hers completely, the bones of his fingers like bars. She's looking down, but can feel his eyes, staring. And he calls her *sweetheart*, saying, "Sweetheart, I'm so sorry." It's all rocks and gravel in his voice. She tries to slip her hands free, but he keeps a firm grip on them. She can sense Lady Bird looking at her. At the mess she is. Already planning to pick out a nice change of clothes. Clean her up. Fix her hair. Maybe run a warm bath. But Lyndon will not let go of her hands. It's as though he wants her to cry before him. But she won't cry. Even if she could.

The compartment is hot and crowded, and it smells of sweat. And she just wishes this would get going. Lyndon finally lets go, and he reaches for a glass of water, swallowing it in one gulp, as though trying to drown himself. Everybody's shifting. Every movement magnified. The judge takes her place, with the Bible in one hand and the typed-out oath in the other. The Dictet is turned on to preserve this moment. Prove that it was real, when nobody will be able to believe such a thing could happen.

Lyndon speaks his lines of the oath slowly; not as though deliberately savoring the moment, rather he's unable to get hold of the words. As though his voice and his brain belong to two different bodies. Judge Hughes seems to rush her part, trying to speed him up.

After Lyndon repeats *So help me God*, there's a pause, a long pause, and it's so quiet in the room, almost without air. This should be the space they stay in forever, where everything just pauses. Lyndon leans down and kisses Lady Bird with his eyes open; and when he catches Jackie's glance, he pulls away from his wife, a little ashamed, reaching out to Jackie, but she doesn't give her hands this time. He hugs her like he's hugging a man, and then takes a half step back, holds on to her elbows. She doesn't want him to say anything, and he seems to know it. He purses his lips, then swallows. Looking at her. Part of her hopes he's sick inside. That his intestines can barely hold anything in. And it's not from anger toward him. Nor from spite. It's just seeing his men behind him shaking hands.

Again, he says, "I am so sorry, Jackie."

"Thank you, Mr. President." As she steps to the side, his hands stay on her elbows, and she realizes that he is in his own pause. Once she feels his hands slip away, she knows everything is moving forward. That there is no place for her, other than to tend to her husband.

If.

It's impossible not to think in terms of *if.* When she'd been walking through the cabin to the swearing-in, she'd considered over a dozen *ifs.* She thought of the weather. The bubbletop. The various pauses along the route, each time Jack commanded the car to slow down to say something to a spectator. Maybe when they motored around the corner into the downtown. If maybe she'd leaned in to say something, and, unable to hear, he'd leaned back just as the bullets passed by. If maybe she'd sat that much closer to him. If maybe the wind had shifted, and the hanging banners had blown in the other direction. Or if maybe she'd pushed the hair off her forehead. Or if maybe Patrick hadn't died.

If was a split second that nearly any detail might have altered.

But already she can't recall details. Only flashbulbs. Snapshots that barely linger. This morning in Fort Worth already is another lifetime. Sitting in the Hotel Texas, getting dressed. Wishing he wouldn't laugh about the risks. Thinking she should say so, because she was that certain something wasn't right. But deciding not to. And when that first shot rang out, and she didn't know what it was, a noise, a firecracker, and Jack's clutching at his throat, and she leaned in toward him. Knew something was wrong. It was barely a second. A breath. But when she leaned over and grabbed at him (asking? yelling? shrieking?), that thought about deciding not to say something went through her head, as though it were loading the bullet and cocking the rifle. She tried to scream it from her mind, just as the next shot came. Then she was climbing out of the car.

But it was the proper thing at the time, right?

As she entered the suite for the swearing-in, she was replaying that second, trying to remember if that's how it had really happened. Not quite certain anymore. Maybe her mind was already recalibrating the details. Turning it into her own private experience, with an ordering of details that at least gave the murder a logic.

Once over the threshold of the room, she looked up to see all those familiar faces staring back at her, and then looking away just as quickly. She tried to lift her head up and walk into the room with pride. But nothing was working right. She tripped on a tuft of carpet, losing her balance. Every hand reached out to brace her. If only she'd paid attention.

Within Twenty-eight Seconds: Part Two.

Lyndon has walked over to talk to his people. Strangely, he already looks presidential. Jack worked hard to make Lyndon feel valued in his vice-presidential role. Inviting him and Lady Bird to state dinners. Making sure each guest was welcomed by both the president and vice president. Jack sent Lyndon abroad, using him as the ambassador that Nixon never was. He'd bungled some early on, especially in Berlin. But Jack had bailed him out. Lyndon just didn't have a diplomat's personality. It's about social ways. But there he is, standing across the room. Already as though he were born into the job.

Lady Bird puts a hand to Jackie's wrist. Her touch is opposite Lyndon's, fragile, like kindling. And Lady Bird's face is sympathetic, maternal, so different from everybody else, who seem frightened of her. "Let's get you away from here," Lady Bird says. "Let me help you."

Words are hard to find. But Jackie tells her thank you.

The two of them stand in the center of the room. Hushed voices surrounding them. Not quite sure where to go.

"We need to get you out of those clothes, dear," Lady Bird says, almost in a whisper. She looks Jackie over. "Get you changed into something more comfortable. Out of these."

Jackie looks down. Her dress is covered in blood. Her right leg caked with it. She reaches up to scratch her cheek and sees her glove almost fully stained brown. She draws in a deep breath, taking in enough air to keep her standing.

"Please, Jackie. Let me help you get changed."

Jackie's not ready to move. Not sure where to go. What to do. And she can sense Lady Bird getting antsy. Trying to find the right things to say. Being helpful. Keep any conversation going, because Lady Bird must be sure that quiet is the worst thing right now. Where the horrors get played and played over and over. But Jackie does want the quiet. Needs it. And she wants it to be with Jack. Sit with him as though these past two hours never existed.

"Shall we go now, Jackie?" Lady Bird's voice starts to tremble.

Together, they walk out of the room and into the hallway, to the bedchamber. Jackie wants to keep moving to the back of the plane. To Jack. But she lets herself be guided. Her thoughts seem like wishes. She's unable to go anywhere she's not directed.

The bedroom is much cooler than the rest of the plane. A streak of blood stains the comforter. There is one dimpled spot on the bed, where Jackie had been sitting before she left for the swearing-in. She sits there again. The mattress barely gives.

Lady Bird again offers to help find a change of clothes. She busily opens the closet door, intruding in a way that she would never do otherwise. "Let's see," she says. The wire hangers ting against each other. Lady Bird doesn't yet know that she's first lady. It hasn't overtaken her the way the presidency has with her husband. She stands with her back to Jackie. Shoulders twitching, breathing rapidly. She too must be suffering, but try-ing not to show it, believing she has no right to.

"We always enjoyed the two of you," Jackie says. "Always enjoyed your company."

Lady Bird is breathing harder. Her wool coat rises and falls. "Now, maybe this one," she says, still looking in the closet. "I'd think this one would be most comfortable." She turns around halfway. Jackie only sees her in profile. And although Lady Bird is talking, it's strange that Jackie doesn't see her mouth moving. Lady Bird is saying that she'll wait right here if Jackie wants to step into the washroom to get cleaned up. She starts to pull a dress off the rack. A simple dark one Jackie had planned to wear to Governor Connally's evening reception. "Then I'll help you get into this," Lady Bird says. "You'll be much more comfortable, dear. Much more."

But Jackie shakes her head. She draws a tight smile, enough to ward off tears. Her chin trembles. And she feels a tingle at the base of her neck. Looking up at Lady Bird, Jackie's head continues to shake. She's pushing away at the dress. "No," she says, and Lady Bird says, "What?" and Jackie says, "I want the world to see what they've done to Jack." And though she'd intended to say it in a way that was appreciative and explanatory, when she hears her own words, floating through the bedroom as though they are somebody else's, she realizes the bitterness and ferocity behind them.

Near Death.

Maybe that's when she thought she was dying.

On the back trunk of the limousine. Accelerating out of parade speed. Screaming. Calling out for Clint Hill. He was screaming back. Climbing on the bumper. Reaching for her hands. Her cries were real. A throaty, primal version of her voice. But the cries were coming from someplace else. A broken version of herself, smashed wires and splintered parts.

Maybe that's when she thought her soul was ascending.

On top of the car. Without heartbeats and pulses. For a moment she seemed so light. All vapor. Where a bullet could pass freely. There were no people. No crowds. No city streets or battlegrounds. Everything seemed oddly perfect.

Maybe she had died for just a moment.

When she and Clint took cover in the car, it was as though she'd fallen back into her body. A strange crash in which nothing seemed to fit right. Shrunken and stretched. And the blood is soaking her, and Jack's pushed down into the seat, his face smashed against the interior, and it stinks and it's raw, and she can hear Clint's heart pounding against her back, and Connally moaning, and she just can't fit back into her body, nor does she want to, because although she keeps talking to Jack, whispering to him that he'll be okay, she knows Jack is dead, and she doesn't want to be in this world anymore. She can't even scream. Her body is refusing her mind. It's all contortions. Closing her eyes, she believes she's crawling out of her body again into a strange world; but when the limousine finally pulls up to the ambulance bay and Clint jumps out, she finds her arms wrapped around Jack, and she knows they're her arms, and she knows just where she is, and what the inside of a human body smells like.

Shock.

At the hospital, the doctor told her it was shock. He was pushing up her sleeve while he topped off the needle, saying shock can do things to the body that you wouldn't think were possible. The body works on its own in traumatic situations, he said, finding its own way to cope with the stress. She hadn't said anything about the experience. She hadn't said anything at all. But he kept talking about shock as though he knew. As nervous around her as all the rest. Trying to provide comfort through logic. The solace of science. He tapped the syringe and rubbed alcohol on her arm. It would take effect in a matter of minutes. Temper the shock. Maybe seconds, even.

All she really wanted was a cigarette. Where she could rise up and drift away with the smoke.

Walking Spanish: Part Two.

Lady Bird looks back once as she leaves the bedroom. Jackie nods, as if to tell her it's fine. She takes in a deep breath. Looks around the room. Rubbing her hand along the comforter on Jack's side.

Everything's over in less than a minute. Less than twenty-four seconds to fire the bullets. Twenty-eight seconds to take the oath. Now she's left sitting here while Jack lies at the other end of the airplane.

She rises. Goes to the door, pushing it open, peeking out to both sides of the main cabin. Without opening it the whole way, she slips through the doorway, almost ghostly. She just wants to be with Jack now. In private. She's done her duty, tried to stand proud for her children and the memory of their father. Now she wants to sit with her husband.

She moves through the cabin, grabbing the seat backs for balance. Startles when she sees O'Donnell standing in front of her. He glances over her shoulder. She hears people.

"Jackie," he whispers, as though it's the third or fourth time he's said it. "Is everything . . . ?"

"I'm just. . . "

"Let me help you."

"I just want to be with Jack."

"The plane's about to . . . Captain Swindal's just announced. Let me help you. Please."

"No. Alone."

"Please let me."

"I just want to be with Jack."

O'Donnell pauses. Looks over his shoulder. "A chair, maybe?"

"A chair would be nice."

"I'll get you a chair. For the living room."

"That would be nice. A chair would be nice."

He walks in front of her, in a nervous rush. Behind her, people are watching. She feels it. An unnatural quiet. A fixed silence. And behind them, the new president will already be on the phone, making plans and arrangements, assuming his position. As soon as she's safely out of sight, the people behind her will join the president. Huddling over him. Making sure his wife is content. But for now they're waiting anxiously. Watching. Their impatient stares pushing her along toward Jack. Through the cabin hallway of Air Force One. Being pushed away. One hand on one seat back at a time. Walking Spanish.

WHAT PROFESSOR TACKACH REMEMBERS

True Story.

They were all just kids in a New Jersey parochial school. And, as he remembers it, Sister Bridget, the principal, who was always so staid and shy, burst into the room, her face gone in a hundred directions, saying, "President Kennedy has been shot in Dallas."

The children were all moved into the chapel in the adjacent church and told to wait and pray. They sat in silence. Only the occasional cough or sniffle. Nervously unsure. But everybody, even the smallest ones, knew their prayers had gone unanswered when the priest came up to the altar dressed in black vestments, looked out over the room, eyes fixed above the crowd like a stage-fraught actor, and said, "Let us pray for the repose of the soul of President John F. Kennedy."

True Coda.

Congressman Patrick Kennedy says there isn't a day when someone doesn't tell him the story of where she was when his uncle Jack was shot. How eager people are to recall their stories, as though after all these years they're still trying to understand them. Still, he tells you, he understands the importance of mythology, and the way in which stories don't just preserve the myths, but help connect them to the larger world. And how sometimes it's the retelling of stories that brings purpose. How placing yourself within them makes something a little less senseless. Patrick Kennedy, who wouldn't be born for another four years after the bullets were fired, has become part of the story.

THE SCIENCE OF WARMTH

THE PHYSICS ARE SIMPLE. Through *thermal conductivity*, energy is transferred from atom to atom, moving heat to otherwise cold places, due to the difference in temperature between them. Fourier's law of heat conduction tells us that the "time rate" of heat flow through the receiving object is proportional to the difference in temperature.

There is a formula for that law.

There is always someone with an answer. For everything.

It is about a five-hour trip by air from Dallas to Washington, and Jackie spends much of it in the rear of the plane, sitting beside the bronze casket that carries her husband's body. Sometimes she places her hand on its top. Her fingers are long and slim, what people usually call *piano hands*. She rests her palm on top of the cold metal casing, testing to see if her body can warm the spot. But she is cold and chilled. The feeling that she has not slept for weeks is coupled by a fear that she probably won't sleep a full night for the rest of her life. Drugs or no drugs. But the spot beneath her hand does warm.

She leans in closer. Maybe the heat is coming from someplace else. It can't be from her.

Biting her lip, Jackie looks up. Scans the room. She wanted privacy, but they check on her anyway. When she is sure that nobody is behind her, Jackie closes her eyes.

Then, leaving her hand on the warm spot of the casket, she cranes her neck down to its side, near the handles, and she whispers, "Jack?"

She holds her breath, imagining. The discovery that this has all been some kind of medical oversight. A terrible misunderstanding that might be laughed about in years to come. At the thought of delivering such news, she can picture standing in the cabin, the stupefied look on Johnson's face, and the delirious panic that would come from O'Donnell and all the other loyalists. How thrilling to be at a loss for those words.

Jackie lets her breath out again.

"Jack?" she whispers, feeling her full voice trying to break through. "Jack?" And she pulls closer to the casket, leaving her hand in place. Where there is warmth there is hope.

Jack's foot had still felt warm when she kissed it. That had been in the emergency room at Parkland, and he had been covered by a sheet that was thick and bulky at the top, from where his head was still wrapped in layers of other sheets. Had he been given last rites? Jackie wanted to know. The priest told her *conditional rites*. There was finality to his voice when he said that. It trembled in his throat. That was when Jackie took off her ring. She turned to leave the room, feeling neither brave, nor proud, nor resigned. She ran her empty finger along the edge of the gurney. The metal, cold and detached, cut a straight line through the stillness of the room. Part of Jack's right foot had been left uncovered. Sticking out. The tendons slightly tensed. His big toe at attention, with the wisp of blond hair curling up. Jackie braced her hands on the gurney. She leaned over. Only her lips touched his foot.

And although it is not rational, this is hope. Sitting in the back of the plane, still tasting the warmth of his foot and feeling the heat emanate off the double-walled bronze casket. Keeping perfectly still. Nothing in her body seems to be moving. Where her gut should be churning and her nerves ought to be leaping, there is nothing. But it is not like a deadening. It is more as though there were no biology inside her. Arms and legs screwed in place. Marbles for eyes. Dreams for thoughts.

She keeps thinking, *Conditional rites. Conditional rites. Conditional rites.* Nothing has been settled yet. Just declarations and signatures and bowed heads and wadded latex gloves and bloodied aprons half hanging in the laundry basket. But there has been no final absolution. No confirmation that God has given up on him. And so long as she feels him on her lips and her hand, she will not be fully resigned.

It is five hours back to Washington.

He was smiling at her less than two hours ago.

They must be over New Mexico. She pictures their route like a cartoon scene; a caricatured map of the United States, divided by the puzzle-shaped pieces, each with a different flower, maybe some livestock, and a star where the state capital is located. And her route is a black line traveling across those states, cutting through time. Part of her wishes the line would turn west. Maybe circle up around the Pacific Northwest, the Redwoods, Puget Sound. Maybe travel south down Highway 1 to Big Sur, Malibu, and San Diego. Then head east, over the Rockies, the Great Lakes, all the way over to the eastern bays—Narragansett, Chesapeake, Cape Cod. This country is too big for a direct route. And although she needs to hold her children, part of her wishes the plane would never land. This is their last time together alone. When that big black line stops at Andrews Air Force Base, she will have to hand Jack over to the country.

Kinetic energy refers to the energy that is produced through motion, the kind that propels a static body into action. Friction occurs when two moving objects come in contact with each other and convert the kinetic energy into sensitive energy, otherwise known as heat.

$Ff = \mu \times N$ is the approximation that Charles Augustin de Coulomb developed to explain friction. A simple and somewhat incomplete approximation, yet adequate enough to explain most encounters.

It seems there is *always* an explanation.

The metal beneath her touch begins to cool. Jackie's instinct is to move her hand back and forth to warm it. But if she does that, then it is only physics at work. She presses her hand down harder. Not to make heat but to find it.

She feels a twinge of panic, which is meaningful only because it shows she can still feel. But then there are those terms like *phantom limb* and *muscle memory*, and again she is not sure what is and what is not real—only that she senses a slight cooling.

Leaning forward even more, she considers calling out for Jack again. But she catches herself. Now she is afraid of the answer.

O'Donnell's presence is startling. In the back of the plane he stands to the side of her, his hands on his thighs, rubbing back and forth against his gray slacks. He stares into the casket wall. A faint outline reflected in the bronze finish. "I know you want to be alone," he starts. And he pauses before the implied *but*.

She blocks him off from the casket. A partial eclipse. She straightens up slightly, still trying to keep an ear close to the seal. Her shoulder blades tense, could cut right through her jacket, sharp and exacting. She leaves her hand on the casket top. Rolls her lips inward, unwilling to give anything away.

"I'm maintaining," she says. He probably can't hear her. With her back to him, it must sound like she's mumbling.

"I can sit back here with you . . . If you would like . . . Only, of course, if you'd like."

She says, "Thank you, but I . . ."

"I'm sorry?"

"I think I prefer to just . . ."

"Sorry?"

Is O'Donnell forcing her to talk louder? She turns slightly, but not enough to move her hand from its place.

"Jackie." He puts his hand on her arm. It is warm. "I know it's crazy to be having this conversation, but we need to think about the funeral." His voice wavers, landing with a strange strength on the word *funeral*.

"It *is* crazy."

"Sorry?"

"I said it *is* crazy. To be having this conversation." She just cannot talk above a whisper.

"It's just that . . ."

"What?"

"That if there are any special plans or services that you would like me to relay to the . . ."

"I can't have this conversation, Kenny."

"We only have until the plane lands before protocol takes everything over."

Jackie looks at him. "It *is* crazy to be having this conversation."

It doesn't appear that O'Donnell hears her. He just nods.

She asks, "What did the Lincolns do?" And the very fact that she asks that question without thinking of it as history astounds her. As if she is talking about the aging couple up the block that she remembers from childhood.

"I'll find out what is transpiring in Washington," he says. "I'll find out . . . Just wait here, and I'll find out."

She nods.

"Okay, then," O'Donnell says. "I'll report back shortly."

When she hears the last of his footsteps, she leans forward. A child whispering under the covers so her parents won't hear, she says, "Jack?" She waits a moment, and then again, a little louder, "Jack?" But she hears only the sound of heat leaving, as if it really is audible.

With O'Donnell gone she can't shake the idea of being connected to the Lincoln family. Lincoln's portrait hangs in the White

House with the same dusty distance of George Washington and Thomas Jefferson, for whom hotels, cities, sales, and elementary schools are named. That strange daguerreotype of Mary Todd Lincoln, cropped into an oval frame, where she poses, dignified, a slight Mona Lisa smile, her plump face turned barely to the right, with her cameo and huge earrings and roses in her hair, the physiognomy of the poor white farmer's daughter with the inherent sophistication of the gentlemen noble class. It's all been history books, no more present than Shakespeare or the great philosophers, ones that she has read over and over. But now Jackie understands the short thread of history. And somehow the stories become more prescient, and she understands how Mary Todd Lincoln folded under the pressure of the assassination, later to be declared officially insane by an Illinois court and, at the insistence of her own son, committed to a sanitarium. This woman of great intellect and poise, who orchestrated her husband's rise and created his mythology within the moments of his life, could not hold on. Suddenly one hundred years is not a long time. Three or four generations at best. If you turn the soil, the bottom layer is still moist.

She stands up, taking her hands off the casket, and turns around to try to catch O'Donnell. She has always been impulsive. Ideas come crashing into her head, and she has to act on them with immediacy or else she loses interest. She calls after him. She calls out, "Kenny," but there's so little power in her voice.

As she walks through the cabin, all the staff stares. Most of their names escape her, and several of the faces are unfamiliar—probably Johnson's people. And though walking seems impossible, instinct is gone—as though her brain has to send detailed instructions to every joint and muscle—under all those eyes she feels the need for poise. She pulls her head up, squares her shoulders, tugging on the hem of her jacket to straighten it, the blood stains like badges. She feels the tone of the room change from pity to respect as she moves through the cabin, searching for O'Donnell, pushed by her vision.

She finds him leaning over a desk, one finger tracing sentences in an open binder, a phone to his ear. He nods an affirmation to Pam Turnure, who, barely twenty-five, must be feeling twice her age. Normally the press secretary to the first lady, on this trip Pam had been directed to devote her time to assisting Mac Kilduff with the president's press duties. It was what Jackie wanted—to direct all the attention toward Jack. Not another Paris. No more sympathy cards. Jackie had come to Texas only to support her husband, the first time she'd traveled with him since his election. *It will be the first of many times,* she'd instructed Pam to say to the media.

Pam excuses herself. Her hip knocks against the chair back. She looks down and mumbles something about being in touch with Nancy in Washington. Jackie can't understand her. All mumbles. Jackie doesn't ask. Personally, she's never been sure how much to trust Pam. But she's always been able to rely on Pam's loyalty to the administration.

O'Donnell closes the notebook and clumsily cuts off his call as the phone slips off his shoulder and lands on the desktop like a hammer. He looks weathered and exhausted, driven only by the need to stay busy.

"Jackie," he says, then glances at a passing staffer and corrects himself. "Mrs. Kennedy. I was just speaking with Sargent

Shriver. He's already working with MDW. They said Jack didn't have any funeral plans in place."

"He's only forty-six, Kenny."

"It just complicates things a bit. They have to create a plan. It's being assigned to . . ." He looks down at his notes. " . . . Major General Wehle. Philip Wehle. There are so many arrangements. So many details."

"Tell Philip Wehle I want him to follow the protocol of the Lincoln procession. Or tell Sargent. Or whomever."

O'Donnell nods. "I did mention it. And Pam's been speaking with Mr. West. The usher staff is working on getting a replica of the Lincoln catafalque for the White House viewing. There's just so much . . ." His voice breaks. He looks so powerless.

"Well," Jackie says, speaking on the exhalation. She knows she's on her own. "Please be sure that I have a book. One that details President Lincoln's procession. I'll brief Sargent. This General Wehle at MDW and anybody else who doesn't understand the level of detail that I intend to see for my husband's funeral. This will not be a slapdash re-creation of text from a policy and procedure manual. This will have the elegance, dignity, and honor that Jack deserves. It is all in the details, Kenny. Each one must be sculpted. Every beat of every song considered."

"I understand, Mrs. Kennedy."

"So, please forward that to Sargent. And have someone gather up all the books about President Lincoln's funeral procession. Immediately, please."

She touches O'Donnell lightly on the shoulder. She doesn't want him to think her angry with him. In some respect, at this particular moment, on an airplane, wandering across the country, without their families and friends, all they have is each other.

Squaring her shoulders, Jackie walks back through the cabin. She holds her chin up and breathes through her nose. It is impossible to swallow.

The sight of the bronze casket is jarring. She has a terrible sense of guilt for leaving Jack's side for even a moment. She puts her hand atop the casket. She doesn't bother saying his name again. But if she did, she would whisper. Explain to him that she needs to think like this. Make these plans. That as much as the world adores them, the world doesn't understand them. All they had ever wanted was to make the extraordinary ordinary. But, she would say, if she doesn't maintain her vigilance they will be lost to mediocrity. It is the natural tendency of the world. She just wants them to burn on forever.

And she'd ask for his patience. His understanding for when she'll call out for Kenny. For Pam. Words that will nearly trip over themselves, tumbling through the door. Calling out. Demanding. *There are plans. There are plans.*

But for now she stays at his side, keeping her hand on the box, believing he can warm her forever. Hoping for something greater than science. Anything that will defy explanation.

HEAVIER THAN AIR

IT'S THE OPPOSITION of pressure that keeps a bird in flight. The air on the top of the wing has a lower pressure than the air on the bottom. That difference is what makes the wing able to lift. This principle is especially important to understanding how tons of steel can stay aloft. Still, it barely makes sense when you really think about it. Floating an object that is heavier than air?

She can sense the plane starting to lower. It is smooth, almost imperceptible. But it's there in her stomach. A sinking sensation. She looks up from the casket toward the window. It's dark already. Maybe someone could set the clock back a few hours. She can't see a thing. Not even her own reflection. But she knows what she looks like. She can smell it. Her body is tired and has sweated out too many rounds of fear, along with the chemicals the doctors have injected into her. She inhales her own toxicity and sees her whole tired frame. The blood on her dress has dried. Already leathered the fabric. A slaughter-house apron. It stinks as such. Nothing is familiar beyond the interior of Air Force One. Not even herself. She smells wrong. Her mouth tastes wrong. Everything is wrong. A big bronze casket wedged in the plane's living room is wrong. This is somebody else's life she's entered. And she wishes the plane would keep flying. Step on the gas, Captain Swindal, drive this thing through some kind of time and space continuum. But don't land yet. Not yet. Not until she gets her life back. Else she'll be stuck with this one forever.

In 1951, when Jackie was twenty-two, she took a job for the *Washington Times-Herald* following her studies at the Sorbonne. She roamed D.C., interviewing people on the streets about issues of the day, photographing them, and running their responses and pictures in her column, Inquiring Camera Girl by Jacqueline Bouvier. The paper gave her $42.50 per week and a Speed Graphic press camera made by the Graflex com-pany. She was told that nothing in the camera was automatic. Pay attention to what you're doing or you'll be shooting out of focus, double exposing, or coming out with blanks. It's not so hard. They told her the camera only looks complicated. Before you know it, you'll be used to it.

It was only two days ago. She was crouching down, her skirt pulled over her knees, a hand on each of her children's shoul-ders. They looked misty-eyed and bewildered as their father hurried around with his usual group of men, talking and read-ing papers at once, pausing for a goodbye that he seemed reluc-tant to say. She gently kissed each of their cheeks. Told them it was a quick trip. Next week would be John-John's birthday and Thanksgiving. Nobody was going anywhere. She sensed worry in their faces. She could not ignore it. The children had every right to be worried. Only three months ago they'd watched her leave for the hospital to have Patrick. She hadn't returned the same. Kneeling in the Cross Hall, she looked them straight on. *We'll be back before you know it*, she thinks she said. *You can trust me*, she thinks she said. *You can trust me*. Then she rose and told them she loved them. The children backed up into Miss Shaw's legs, leaning against their nanny like she was a wall, as they watched their mother back away, bent forward and blowing kisses. Then she turned around and walked a pace behind Jack, feeling less and less like a mother.

Now she would have to tell them everything would be all right.

How could they ever trust her again?

Pam Turnure barely knocks, but it sounds like thunder. Jackie tells her to come in. The supposed younger version of herself. The subject of rumor and innuendo. She could hate her and blame her. Accuse her. Believe that it was Pam whom she associated with the feminine smells on her husband's body. But Pam enters the living room in loyalty and service. Willing to hide the heartbreak. Her notebook tucked under her arm. Mascara hastily mobbed in the corners of her eyes. Pam stands to the side of the casket. Licks her lips. "Yes, Mrs. Kennedy?" she says. "Yes?"

"You need to call Maud Shaw right away," Jackie says.

"Call Maud Shaw."

"She'll have to tell the children tonight. I'll see them in the morning. I'll be back so late. But they need to know. Miss Shaw needs to."

Pam stands silent. Swallows. Puts the tip of her pen on the notepad. "So they should receive the news from Miss Shaw?"

"That's what I've said."

"She'll ask what she should say. What would you like her to say?"

"Tell her to tell them that Johnson did it."

"Mrs. Kennedy?"

"Or God."

"I can't."

"Can't what?"

Pam says nothing. She makes as though she's going to write, but the pen rests lazy in her hand.

Jackie closes her eyes, sucking in a breath. It lingers in her stomach, swelling it. "Miss Shaw can tell them that the same God who took Patrick also called for his father. That God knew Patrick would be lonely in heaven. That his father was needed to look after him because he needed a best friend." And in principle and faith, she believes that statement. But for right now it is only a series of words. Each as weightless as the next.

A smaller bird uses all her excess energy to keep warm. She is designed to keep a sophisticated flow of energy in her body while maintaining her lightness. Her skeleton is hollow to reduce weight; and, in the course of her evolution, she has lost all unnecessary bones.

The Graflex camera ended up being easier to use than she'd expected. Jackie stopped thinking about the mechanics of the range finder or the shutter options, instead opting to focus on the composition of each picture in collaboration with the words.

Initially, she'd almost taken a job at *Vogue*, debated and deliberated, but ultimately found the *Washington Times-Herald* more appealing. There was the allure of the man on the street. Washington socialites. Politicos. They all talked to her. Pat Nixon. Vice President Nixon. Senator Kennedy. Senator Kennedy again. And again. She never stopped her work. Wandering the capital's streets. The parties. Overseas to England to cover the coronation of Queen Elizabeth. The *Times-Herald* was where she cut her teeth. Negotiated the demureness of the obedient debutante with the confidence of the grown woman. It was where she learned how the quiet in her voice could carry its own strength.

After she arrived back from London, Senator Kennedy proposed to her. She'd known this day was coming from the first night they'd met. She'd been charmed by him, and suspicious of him, but wasn't that every man? Four months later they're on the sidewalk on Spring Street in Newport, Rhode Island, just married. In the sunlight and cheer, the homely St. Mary's Church sits as a backdrop, having found its good looks. And she's wearing a silk dress with a portrait neckline, and a bouffant skirt banded by over fifty yards of flounces. Jack starts to say something to her. She looks at him through the same veil that her mother wore at her own wedding, then adjusts her pearl choker, mouthing, *What?* He says it again, but she still can't hear. There are more than eight hundred people streaming around them, and the cameras are flashing, and as they are heading for their car, she thinks that once she gets him alone she'll be able to hear what he is trying to say to her. But they're off to the reception at the Auchincloss estate, where there are an additional four hundred guests, and a wedding cake nearly as tall as she; and it's hard to hear anything amid the conversations. In their one free second, she says, "What did you say to me in front of the church?" and just when he leans over to speak, Meyer Davis starts up the orchestra, and the horns are competing with the drums, and then she and Jack are paraded out on the dance floor, and immediately congratulated by every twirling couple around them. Then it's down to Acapulco, and up to Montecito, and by then she's forgotten to ask what he said, taken in by all the sights and the gangs of friends and family members and associates that appear in the corners of every circumstance. Before she knows it they are back in Georgetown, and they're sitting at the breakfast table before a morning session, and she looks at him and says, "Jack, what were you trying to say on that sidewalk? At our wedding. As we were leaving St. Mary's." He considers, and then smiles. The smile turns to a laugh that rocks his shoulders. She is laughing too, but she doesn't know why. Finally, he takes in a breath, then exhales with a light whistle. "The thing is," he says, "I can't remember right now." He starts gathering papers into his satchel. "You'd think it was so long ago, these past weeks. And I just can't remember. But I will. I will."

That was in September of 1953, and since then she's never stopped. A decade straight through. Campaigns. Children. Back and forth across the country. Across the world. Empty beds. Unfamiliar perfumes. Never even a pause.

And now, as the plane is set to land, it seems as though she might be stopping for once. After more than ten years running.

She is guilty with relief. It's only a pause. But, still, she feels the relief.

The plane bends, making a slight turn to the right. The pull of the earth is stronger. Pam starts to back out of the room. An elongated version of her face reflects off the bronze casket. Jackie says, "Wait, please," and Pam stops. Looks right at her, mouth slightly open, looking every bit as callow as her twenty-odd years would suggest. "Mrs. Kennedy?" she says. "Mrs. Kennedy?"

"It's too soon for the plane to land."

Pam stands still.

"You'll have to tell Captain Swindal. You'll have to tell him I don't want him to land the plane."

Pam doesn't move. She leans forward, rubbing the tips of her fingers together. "I think it's too late, Mrs. Kennedy. Too late for that."

Jackie pushes down on her ring finger, twisting, as though the ring were still there. "I don't know," she says. "There is still so much to plan. We need to take hold of the details. We need time, Pam."

Pam starts to sit but stops, knees buckled. She has not been invited. She hugs her notepad against her chest.

"Has anyone talked with Mr. West yet? What has he found out? In the White House Library, Pam. There is a book. It has illustrations of the White House while President Lincoln was lying in state. Somebody needs to find that. And they need to get that book to William Walton. He'll know how to reproduce the drapings for the East Room. W-A-L-T-O-N. But somebody needs to be doing that—getting the book. Getting it to him. Is Mr. West doing that?"

"Let me check, Mrs. Kennedy."

"That's what I mean. We don't have enough time. There's no time for checking. How can we be landing already?"

"My understanding is that under Mr. West the White House ushers are working on everything. Schlesinger and Goodwin are also at the Library of Congress tracking down information on the Lincoln funeral."

"Yet we still need to pack. Pack up the plane. We can't just leave Jack's things here, Pam. Somebody needs to make sure. Will you make sure?"

"I will, Mrs. Kennedy."

"But you don't have the time."

"The flight crew will see to it."

"I don't want the flight crew. It's not cleanup. I wish Mary could pack. But she doesn't have the time. We don't have the time. Don't you feel the wheels dropping, Pam? Don't you?"

O'Donnell comes into the room to tell Pam that Mr. West is on the telephone. West has one question, a single one that he hopes to have answered before the plane lands. O'Donnell apologizes for the intrusion. He explains, "It's just that West sounded urgent."

Pam looks to Mrs. Kennedy, who says, "Take it. And please call Miss Shaw. For the children."

Pam nods. She starts to turn. Tries to look assured. At least convey some confidence. But as she exits the room Pam is slightly hunched, shoulders slouched. Her skirt is off center, tugged slightly to the right.

O'Donnell walks along the walls, as though avoiding any potential contact with the casket. Ending up by the cupboard, where the glasses and liquor are kept, he looks over at Jackie. They'll be landing soon, he says. She just nods. "Maybe a scotch before we touch down," he suggests. She says, "You know I've never had a scotch in my life." He tells her, "Now might be as good a time as any."

He says he'd better take his seat for the touchdown. He understands by now that she prefers to be left alone. As he starts to leave, she says, "Kenny," and he stops still. She drops her face into her hands. They are sticky. She wants to cry but she's all cried out. That alone seems impossible, that the body could dry itself out. "Maybe just ask Captain Swindal how far he thinks we could go?"

"How far we could go?"

"If we just kept flying. How far we'd get."

O'Donnell looks confused, as though he wishes he could answer the question for her. Instead he says he'll ask. That's all he can do, he says. Just ask.

"I'm not suggesting we hijack the plane," she says. " I only want to know."

It is more than the pressure against the airfoil of her wings that keeps a bird in flight. It is the overall design of her body. As though every cell were built and mutated for that very task. There is the contour of her torso. Small and sleek. The carefully placed organs, calibrated in their rhythms for maximum efficiency. Above all there is lightness. Her feathers almost weightless, light but strong, pliable yet tough. And her bones also are very light. Fused together to reduce the need for muscle. But make no mistake. A bird's bones are solid. Yet constructed in a way to keep her thin and light.

The engines have been cut, and suddenly everything is still. Although she is alone, and although the door is closed, the scuttle of the political operation goes on just beyond her. Tamping feet under growling orders.

This truly is their last moment together. It feels vague. Almost without sentiment. Just a fact to note. In minutes they'll exit out the rear of the plane, into the glare of cameras and newsmen and staff, onto a tarmac that looks oddly vacant, as though it is a stage set artificially lit with not-quite shadows. Everyone there will be unsure of how to look at her, not knowing what should or shouldn't be said. She'll only walk alone for a few seconds before Bobby will rush up the stairs of the truck lift to take her hands. He'll accompany her to Bethesda Naval Hospital and then take her and the body back to the White House. She'll keep her head bowed, and she'll say she's fine, and he'll say, *You don't have to say anything*, and she'll think she wasn't planning on it anyway. There will be hordes around her, the Secret Service escort, the Navy Honor Guard, all working with a confused urgency about how to lift the casket down, a few feet off the truck and into the back of the gray hearse. She'll trail behind until she too has to come off the edge of the truck, and there will be hands on her elbows and wrists. Somehow she will land.

In her final time alone with the casket, she should say something, bear it significance. But there is nothing to say, and even if there were, she wouldn't be able to say it. For this moment, this one single moment, she is glad to live in a world without words. Free from symbols and meanings. Without them, anything is possible. Although grounded by her own weight, she can just touch her hand to the casket and still be flying, high above the darkness and the gravity that holds her there. In flight. Watching herself trudge through every wretched minute, as though each one of those minutes were a day in and of itself. Gliding above. Looking down in sympathy and empathy.

Imagine that. Floating above it all. Heavier than air.

MRS. KENNEDY IS COMING BACK

WE PASS EACH OTHER IN WHISPERS. The White House halls are quiet. The kitchens are quiet. The lights are dimmed. We are all quiet, passing each other in whispers. Miss Shaw says she doesn't think the children should have to see the casket in the East Room, once it finally arrives. "Well how you going to do that?" William asks. "Mrs. Kennedy won't allow for that." And Miss Shaw says, "I'm only saying what I think. It's just my opinion." She keeps walking. Miss Shaw has the children to attend to.

We don't know if she's even told them yet. We don't even know how you tell children such a thing. And there isn't one of us who doesn't pity Miss Shaw the responsibility, but we all are thankful that it wasn't us that got the call. It was Wade who'd said he might have quit if he'd been asked. "Charged," Lucinda said. "Charged. You wouldn't be *asked*. You'd be charged."

"Well, I don't know that I could follow through with it, is all I'm saying. Charged or asked."

"Then you'd have to go. Insubordination."

"I just don't know how you tell that to a five-year-old girl and a two-year-old boy."

"Three," Lucinda said. "Three years old the boy is, for all practical purposes. He's got a birthday just days away."

Wade said, "Now don't get mad at me now, Lucinda. I just can't imagine it. Can't imagine I could ever handle it. That's all I'm saying."

"Well, it's a good thing you're a butler, then."

"Now don't you get mad at me, Lucinda. Don't get mad at me now."

But we're all a little bit mad now. Upset. Paralyzed. Double-checking things like the weather, the clocks, each other. Making sure that this is real. And, swear to God, if we weren't seeing each other's expressions, none of us would believe this was true. That's when we start getting mad. As if the confirmation is the cause. Not some crazy man across the country. But we can't get mad at Miss Shaw. She's doing what none of us ever could. That poor woman must be sick with anticipation. Just waiting. Waiting. We're all waiting. In a big old empty house. Just waiting. In whispers.

Someone asks when Mrs. Kennedy is coming back. None of us knows, but William says the ushers are decorating the East Room. He doesn't say what for. He doesn't need to. But the word is she'll be coming home when that's ready. Wilma says she's nervous about seeing Mrs. Kennedy. That she's afraid she'll lose her composure in front of the first lady, and she'll be so embarrassed because she knows she'll have no right to grieve harder than the widow.

William says, "No offense, Wilma, but it's not as if she'll know you. I mean, no offense to all of you if you think she'll be looking for you. Or even knowing who you are, for that matter."

Most of us do take offense at that comment, and we say so. We may not know much about much right now, but we do know that Mrs. Kennedy knows who we are. And Cordenia looks to have especially taken offense to the comment. She's usually the last among us to start in, but we see her shifting, kicking her feet around. Clearing her throat. Pulling on her sleeves. "That's not a whole truth," she says.

"What's that, Cordenia? I barely hear you."

"I said, that's not quite a whole truth."

"What's not the truth?"

"What he said. About Mrs. Kennedy not knowing. She knows. First day I met her she knew. Right here on the second floor. Right outside the president's bedroom there. Dusting. Mrs. Kennedy walked right up to me and says, 'I don't believe I've met you before. You're new?' And I was so surprised that she'd know me from the rest. I didn't think people of their kind noticed. But she was good to me. Asked me questions. Talked to me. Called me by name."

William says, "That's because you babysat for the children when Miss Shaw took her days off. That's different."

"But I didn't at the time."

"It's different, and you know it."

Cordenia mutters to herself that it's not different, and then says out loud, "You'll see. When Mrs. Kennedy arrives, you'll see." She stands there holding her ground, but we can see that every inch of her self wants to be walking away, shrinking away. She's done proving. Yes, the Kennedys had taken her on their vacations to sit with the children. And, yes, Mrs. Kennedy may have called for her in a way that she didn't call for the rest of us. But Cordenia is still one of us, and she knows it. At the end of the day, she's still a maid going home to an apartment that could fit into the White House a hundred times over.

"You think Miss Shaw has told the children yet?" Wade asks.

How would we know? None of us has moved since we gathered here. In these quiet halls. And that quiet is what beats on us. But Wade's just talking. Keeping things moving. Trying to be normal. Because we know when Mrs. Kennedy comes home nothing will be the same. Right now it's just talk and wonder. But when she comes home, she'll come home alone. And though Wade keeps on asking things he knows we don't have the answers for, we just let him keep on. We don't really want anything concrete right now. We just want to wonder.

She'd never say it out loud, but Miss Shaw must wish today had been her day off. She might have been running some personal errands. Stopping off for a pot of tea in Georgetown. A light lunch when she felt her stomach growl. Maybe she would've heard the news then. Word rippling through the restaurant. Until it built a force that knocked her from her seat. Surely it would've taken an inexorable amount of time to get back to the White House and the children. Cordenia would've been there. She's the one who would've had to take the double blow, to look into the children's eyes as she simultaneously processed the news. Cordenia would've been the one. And maybe the traffic would have been heavier than Miss Shaw expected. In the grief and confusion, people would take to the streets. Pour out of restaurants. Shoe stores. Bookstores. Offices. Filling the buses. Flagging the taxis. Stopping up the avenues.

In that case, then, Cordenia would be the one to get the call from Air Force One, instead, Pam Turnure saying she's presumed Cordenia's heard the news, and it would be Cordenia who wouldn't know what Pam was talking about, forcing Pam to explain what had just happened, and that the first lady needs her service. It would be Cordenia who would swallow, choking back any indication of ambivalence. Holding her breath to keep her stomach down before replying, *Of course, and how else can I be of duty to Mrs. Kennedy?*

It would have been Cordenia.

Instead, Miss Shaw had been sitting in the boy's room, sewing. Caroline was with a friend in the country, John was napping. Perfect silence. No radio. The hallway was quiet; the staff knew he was sleeping. She sat in her chair, legs crossed, the fabric spread across her lap. Drawing the needle along the seam in a backstitch, two forward and one back. Only the sounds of the thread rolling off the spool and John's whistling breaths. Barely hearing the footsteps padding down the second-floor hallway. Stopping at the doorway, John's Secret Service man, Bob Forester, leaned around the corner. She put her finger to her lips. The needle touched just underneath her nose. But he looked insistent, so she started to move her materials off her lap in order to stand and take him into the hallway, where he could say whatever it was he had to say, but still in a whisper, of course. But Bob stepped farther into the room. He said she had a phone call. Before she could protest, looking over at the sleeping boy, Bob said he was ordered to stand guard over the boy until she returned. But she needed to go take the call now. It was a matter of national urgency. And when she picked up the phone, she initially heard strings of static and buzzing. Finally, Pam Turnure's voice filtered through. "Miss Shaw," she said, "I presume you've heard the news."

We don't like to start things that shouldn't be started, but sometimes William does. It's his nature. Because William's skin is so light, he believes that some of the people talk to him a little more than they do to the others. It was reinforced for him downstairs, when an usher told him that Mrs. Kennedy was not coming back until the early hours of morning. She had decided to go to the naval hospital in Bethesda and wait there until they were ready to bring the president home. William heard this downstairs, right before he passed by the East Room. He'd been down there to verify some instructions from Mr. West about which rooms to prepare for the Kennedy family members who were on their way to Washington. That's when he started talking with the usher.

See. I told you so. They just talk at me because they think I'm white. We tried to tell William that had nothing to do with it. Especially today. People around here are so tensed up inside that they'll talk with anybody just to let a little of it out. He didn't buy that. Still, he learned that Mrs. Kennedy is keeping control over everything, despite being in such a bad way. Every effort being done is according to her planning. Right now, the main focus is in preparing the East Room for President Kennedy, but William tells us that we'd better be prepared to host more than just the Kennedy family. Visitors are going to be coming from all over the world.

We nod.

Did you hear me? he asks.

We do. But we want to know what the East Room is looking like. What they're doing to it.

William pauses, says he only saw it briefly. It's not that he didn't want to stare, but he was afraid to. A whole crew was moving things and sweeping and hanging black bunting and working so efficiently. But they were like ghost cleaners, William says. Like he could see right through them. And their feet didn't make a sound. Imagine. In that big empty room with the hardwood floors. Not so much as an echo. But most striking was the big stand in the middle that he figured was there to hold the casket. William says it must be eight feet long, all draped in black. When he looked at it, he saw the portrait of George Washington with a hand outstretched, as though pointing right at the stand. He knows it sounds stupid to say, but he really did pinch himself to see if he was dreaming. He's got a small mark on his forearm to prove it. He couldn't look into the East Room but for a minute, because he says it had started to make him feel ghostly, himself, and he says he broke out into as much of a run as one could have done politely, not stopping until he found us.

Miss Shaw is at the end of the hall. Moving slowly. She stops briefly and looks back at us, over her shoulder. We look at her sympathetically. We know that loyalty and courage don't always mix.

"Maybe Mrs. Kennedy will be home in time," Wilma says. It's a doubtful whisper. "She probably wants to be with her children, anyways."

"I told you," William says, "she won't be back until early morning."

"What do they do at the hospital that takes so long?"

William shrugs. "I don't know. I suppose they're getting his body ready for the casket. Maybe doing an autopsy for the record? Signing on the death certificate."

His matter-of-fact tone stuns William more than us. He tries to backtrack a little, saying that he really doesn't know, it was just based on what he'd seen in movies. And that's the thing: it *is* like a movie, only one that we're inside of. It's as though we see the sets and the artifice surrounding us, but are caught in its drama. We don't know what to believe. Or expect. Some of us are still fully convinced that President and Mrs. Kennedy will walk right up these stairs, looking as inspired as the day they left, just a little bit wearied from the travel.

Cordenia likes to tell this story, about when she first met President Kennedy. She was babysitting John for the first time, and he was crying like nothing, finding himself with this strange person. Cordenia's looking all around for something to entertain the boy, to distract him. And she finds a jack-in-the-box that plays "Pop Goes the Weasel," and, of course, the clown jumps out on the last note. That hushes little John up, so she plays it again. Winding it up again and again. And when she tries to take a break, the boy looks at her, looks at the box, and says, *More*. Cordenia is sprawled out on the floor, barely half turned to the doorway, when the president comes in, and, as honest as sunshine, she has no idea who he is. Even when he starts singing the ending of "Pop Goes the Weasel," just before the clown pops up. The boy is so taken by the clown that he hardly notices his father. The president says hello to Cordenia, and she says hello without turning around, a little tentatively, already feeling a sense of protection over John. She can feel the president standing firm. Still looming. *Who are you?* he asks. *Are you new?* She replies simply, *Yes, I am new.* She's keeping her attention on the boy, who is gesturing to the jack-in-the-box for more. *Did we hire you or did the White House hire you?* She thinks she may have sounded a little snippy when she replied that she was afraid the White House hired her. As she ends the sentence, her mind stops on how he said the word *we*. She'd just finished winding up the toy, and the music has started, and John is clapping his hands. The way the president said *we* made it all clear, and Cordenia says it was like she was seeing the room as a photograph—sprawled out across the floor, with President Kennedy standing over her, watching her body trying to recompose itself.

Miss Shaw must know it would be cruel of her to tell the children before dinner. They'll need their strength. But it will be impossible to look at them eating as though everything is normal. Caroline will talk about her day. John will fly his hand around like an imaginary helicopter, saying, "La-pa-ca. La-pa-ca." While normally she would instruct him on manners, tell him to focus on his meal, tonight Miss Shaw will allow him to play. Be unusually lenient. Hope he doesn't notice; hope that neither asks when their parents are coming home.

William says he hates to think like this, "But do you think we'll still have jobs after today?"

Wade says, "They still have to run the White House, don't they?"

"But Mr. and Mrs. Johnson are likely gonna be having their own ideas in mind," William says. "Their own ways of how they'll be wanting things run."

"Even so, that doesn't mean they have to hire a new staff."

"Maybe yes," William says. "Maybe no."

We bring up how inappropriate it is to be having this discussion. Knowing Mrs. Kennedy is sitting all alone at the hospital, losing her husband the way she did, probably feeling like she's lost everything. We think it best to go about making a comfortable setting for her, once she returns. Putting our focus there. Not thinking about ourselves. Not concerning our thoughts with how we might be affected.

William looks a little flustered. In our hearts we can forgive him, given today's tension. But it's not so easy with our nerves on end. He says he agrees with what we're saying, and that he's insulted we'd find him insensitive. "Still," he says, "I've got a family too. I don't know how these Johnsons are. I don't know what they will or will not be wanting. I mean, do you? Any of you?"

Cordenia starts to raise her hand, holding it tight to her chest, not much above her shoulder. "I met Mr. Johnson once," she says. Cordenia pauses. Looks down to the ground. Her voice is low, barely audible. But she seems taken aback by it. She doesn't notice us looking at her. Waiting.

"And?" William asks. "Well?"

Cordenia's head stays bowed.

"Speak."

She raises her eyes, just enough to meet his. "I guess there's not much to tell. It was last August. In Hyannis Port. He was there with Mr. Rusk. They were on their way overseas."

"That's not telling us much, Cordenia."

"I guess there's not much to tell."

William says, "I'm talking about working for him, Cordenia. Not just seeing him."

"Well, he was nice enough to the children. Polite to me, too. He's louder than President Kennedy, though. I remember that. Louder."

William shakes his head. "All I can say is that you'd better watch out. Get yourself planning tonight. This is a different man about to come in here. Different wife. There won't be no children running through the hallways. No classrooms upstairs. None of us can say what it is, but you can be sure it'll be different. On that you can plan. And I don't know about you, but I'm not counting on myself fitting in to that. Not especially when the only information I've got on Mr. Johnson is that he's *louder than the president*."

We might have told William to move along. That we wanted no part of this conversation or attitude. But maybe we know that part of what William is saying is right. The president and his wife have made us feel like part of their family, part of their circle, making us forget that most of us work for the White House, not for them. But maybe William is altogether right. Once Mrs. Kennedy takes the children out the White House doors for good, this will all just be a story we tell. One that we'll all remember a little differently. About how we used to know the Kennedys.

Helicopters are coming and going from the White House lawn. Each time one arrives, John says, "La-pa-ca. La-pa-ca." He goes to the window, cupping his tiny hands against the glass and then looking back to Miss Shaw. "Daddy? Home. Daddy's home?" he asks. She shakes her head and tries to smile.

Caroline has looked suspicious since she was brought back from the country. She was scooped up and taken home with barely a word. Then the Bradlees showed up at the White

House. Playing with them in the Oval Room. Chasing John around the house. And the helicopters keep coming and going. "La-pa-ca. La-pa-ca." And Caroline tries to look normal, politely telling Mrs. Bradlee about her day. Then her grandparents Auchincloss arrive, and her grandmother announces they'll be having dinner at their house, and that Miss Shaw will meet them back at the White House. And everybody is too nice. Too normal. As though there's no space between their gestures.

Miss Shaw can see that Caroline knows something is wrong. Maybe doesn't know, rather senses. But she hasn't asked a single question. Maybe she's afraid of what she might hear. Maybe she's detected the subtlest nuance that Miss Shaw has been trying to hide—sucking in short breaths, telling herself to project normalcy and calm, when John looks out the window again, saying, "Daddy's home?"

We can't seem to move. Though there is work to be done, we don't have the will. Or maybe it's that none of us wants to be alone. Instead, we all prefer to stand here in the hallway and shake our heads. We've heard people are trying to get into the White House. Just to find out what's going on. See if they can help. But the White House police have closed off all the entrances, and we hear that they're having to monitor every gate, telling each person that everything that can be done is being done, and that someone from the White House certainly will call if assistance is needed. William wants to know, "What people? What kind of people are just showing up at the gates thinking we can use their help?"

"Government people, I'd guess," Lucinda says. "People who have business here."

"I was thinking it was just regular folks. Just coming and banging on the door."

"That'd be okay if it was, don't you think? William, don't you think it'd be a good thing that regular folks want to help out with a kind like the Kennedys? Don't you think that's a good thing, William?"

William looks down. His toe grinds into the carpet like it's the one doing the thinking. "So long as they don't really think anybody will take them on. Just as long as they understand it's only a gesture." And what he doesn't say is that's the reason why we're here. The true representatives of the people. Although it will be menial work—sweeping, dusting, changing linens, serving food—we understand that we're the ones called on to help out in any way we can. And as difficult as William can be, we can all see his point, and share in his pride.

William says, "I suppose we ought to get to work. It's what we're here for. Certainly not family."

We nod our heads. But none of us go. We just wait here, as we've been doing for some time. Milling. Waiting for something. Like all those folks out in Lafayette Park, out there gathered in small circles, stunned and feeling useless. Maybe they're some of the ones coming up to the gates. The ones asking how they can help. They just need someone to tell them what to do. Give a little direction. And, we suppose, that's our story, also. We just need someone to tell us what to do.

William shoves his hands into his pockets and backs up into the group, not saying anything more. Occasionally one of our voices might rise high above the rest, but then it falls back. Maybe that's a good thing. Maybe it's bad. But none of us ever really speaks to each other. We just speak *for* each other.

And together we wait. Waiting for someone to tell us what to do.

We pity Miss Shaw the burden.

She's just come down the stairs from the third floor, on her way to the first. As she passes, someone says, "Godspeed to you, Maud."

Miss Shaw stops and looks back. Her body is staid. Solid and sure. But her eyes look stunned. Almost as though she is blind. "The children are here," Miss Shaw says. "They've just come back from Mr. and Mrs. Auchincloss's house. They're downstairs now."

"The children love you, Maud."

"I don't question that."

"We just want you to know that we understand, Maud."

She says, "Thank you," and starts to walk away. Then she turns around. "Some of you remember the hamsters Caroline had, I imagine. Particularly the little mother that was with her young, separated from the others, as was proper. When the president came in, he looked at her all alone and said that he wanted the male to be put in the cage. We said it was too soon. But he insisted, saying that everybody needs a mate, no one should have to be alone. So we put the male back in—much too soon, I'll remind you—and the male nearly clawed her to death, while she lay still, protecting her children."

Then William, of all people, says he remembers a saying from the ancient Greeks. He'd heard it in church. It's a rule. A guideline. "Assist a man in raising a burden," he says to us more than to Miss Shaw, "but do not assist him in laying it down."

She nods. And while we want to believe in this moment that we all shoulder the burden, we still know that Miss Shaw will be alone in that room. She can take as much of our spirit as she can manage, but when it comes down to it, she'll be the one facing those children. By itself, that thought makes us mourn.

"John and Caroline are downstairs," she says. "They're waiting for me. They're waiting." She stares right at us, but she still looks blind.

"Godspeed to you, Maud. Godspeed."

One voice. But all our voices.

They were the only two in the room, but as we understand it Miss Shaw could barely look at Caroline, tucked firmly in bed under the canopy of rosebud chintz, forcing a confident expression, though it was clear she knew something wasn't right; and Miss Shaw's eyes were tearing while Caroline stared at her, almost demanding an explanation other than Miss Shaw taking her hand and apologizing for the tears; and Miss Shaw knew she could wait until morning (Mrs. Auchincloss told her Mrs. Kennedy said it was up to her to gauge what the children did or didn't know), but she looked at Caroline and something told her it wouldn't be fair to send the girl to sleep, to let her wake up full of promise—better for the girl to wake up as part of the grief, and that way maybe she'll mourn more purely; then Miss Shaw inhaled so deeply her gut almost burst, and on the exhalation she said that there had been an *accident*; then she paused, realizing the sound of hope in the word *accident*, and corrected herself to say, "He's been shot, and God has taken him to Heaven because they couldn't make him better in the hospital," and then closed her eyes, praying that when she opened them she wouldn't see Caroline crying—that this had all been a dream.

If there's any spot of pleasure in this day, it's in looking at William's face. He's just delivered the news that all of us are invited to a mass for President Kennedy, being held in the East Room in the morning. Apparently the invitation has come from Mrs. Kennedy herself, and she's also extended the invitation to our family members and friends. There was humbleness in William's expression as he told us. He spoke softly.

We were tempted to put it back in his face, all his commentary about how the Kennedys don't care about the servants. If he thinks working under them is bad, he should've seen it during Eisenhower, when the servant's place was not to be seen and not to be heard. When President Kennedy first got here, he had been walking down the hallway with an aide, and two of us were vacuuming, and because of having worked for Eisenhower, we knew to shut off the vacuum cleaners and turn to face the wall until he passed. After President Kennedy had walked a little farther on, we heard him whisper, "What is that all about?" *William, we want to say, there wasn't so much as an invitation for us to breathe before President Kennedy got here.* That's what we're tempted to put in William's face. *Not so much as an invitation.*

Some glance at Cordenia to see if she looks vindicated, but she stays poker-faced. There's already enough shame going through William.

We don't need to say anything. Nor will we ever.

Tomorrow morning we'll all go to the mass. We'll stand side by side with each other, and shoulder to shoulder with others from the White House, praying over the president's body. We know we'll have to leave early, maybe only get to hear the beginning, because we'll have to prepare the breakfast, polish the silver, serve the food, and clean up afterward. But we'll be there tomorrow morning as it starts, once President and Mrs. Kennedy have come back.

Until then, we'll work into the early hours.

Line up kerosene lamps spaced out evenly along both sides of the driveway.

Drape the North Portico in black crepe, hanging from ladders, in full view of the people standing outside the gates.

We'll sweep the East Room.

Clean the hallways.

Prepare the bedrooms.

Set the State Dining Room.

And look after the children. Refusing to leave their sides until their mother comes home. On a chair at the side of the bed. Watching out the window, while the clouds fill in the sky, and the last ray of moonlight can still light the room.

BREAKING AND CRUMBLING FROM THE SEVENTEENTH FLOOR
(facts & stories)

A Wearied Sleep.

As the story goes, when Fleetwood Lindley of Springfield, Illinois, died in 1963, he was the last living person to have seen Abraham Lincoln's remains. That was in 1901, when Fleetwood Lindley was only thirteen years old. There had been several attempts to steal the president's body for ransom, and Robert Lincoln, the sole survivor, decided it was best to encase the casket ten feet deep, under a metal cage and a layer of concrete, making it forever impossible to reach. After some debate, it was decided that the remains should be checked before the casket was permanently entombed. There were still rumors and claims that Lincoln's body had vanished long ago. So on September 26, 1901, Leon Hopkins, a plumber, and his nephew, Charles Willey, were charged with opening the casket in front of twenty-three witnesses. Fleetwood Lindley's father, who understood the historic significance, had pulled his son out of school for the occasion. There they stood before the pine casket, in a room with the windows papered shut, while Hawkins and Willey knocked their crowbars against the floor, testing their strength before going to work. When the upper part of the casket was opened, Fleetwood Lindley was sickened by the smell. But once he gathered the courage to look, he couldn't stop staring at the corpse. The brown complexion, pasted white by the undertaker's chalk. Lincoln's trademark beard was still intact, the whiskers poking out from the chin. The familiar mole in place. Instantly recognizable. The only noticeable change was that the president's eyebrows seemed to have disappeared completely. But maybe most memorable to Fleetwood Lindley was Lincoln's melancholy air, which suggested a wearied sleep. Somehow he'd expected to see an expression of shock, from the surprise of a bullet going through the brain.

Polished.

At about 5:00 PM the ambulance left Andrews Air Force Base, headed for the Bethesda Naval Hospital. The sirens were screaming. Lights blazing. Along with the president's remains, the car ferried Jackie, Bobby Kennedy, and the president's physician, Admiral George Burkley, who had been in the second car in Dallas. Off in another direction, a man was dispatched to the White House to bring back one of Jack's suits and a pair of shoes. He told himself to remember to make sure the shoes were polished. President Kennedy wouldn't accept anything less.

It's Mandatory.

The issue of the autopsy had come up while Air Force One had been in flight, somewhere between the swearing-in and the planning of the funeral. Jackie is sitting by the side of the casket, her voice just above a murmur. Maybe she's humming, it's a long and slow melodious howl that vibrates from her chest. She's been trying to think, not about anything in particular, just think, wanting to organize a thought in order to find some footing. The rumble of the airplane unsettles her, but she tries not to think of that. The physics of flight requires too much trust.

She pretends not to see Pam and Kenny come into the room. They won't leave. Kenny puts two fingers on her shoulder. She thinks they might break right through her bones. He says that Dr. Burkley needs to speak with her, and she turns around, about to say, *It takes two of you to tell me?* But she nods, seeing the White House physician waiting in the doorway.

"Mrs. Kennedy," Burkley says, "I'm sorry to bother you at such a time." He glances down for a moment, but then raises his stare, drawing it right into her eyes. "I don't know how to be anything but frank here." He pauses. Looking for her response.

She nods. Her whole world is now frank.

"We're going to have to do an autopsy," he says. "When we get back to Washington."

She shakes her head. "That won't be necessary."

"I'm afraid it's mandatory."

"Well, I say it doesn't have to be done."

"It's mandatory," he repeats, and looks up at Pam and Kenny, as though for assistance. As though she is too dumbstruck to notice.

"I don't know," she says. "I don't know."

"We can do it at Walter Reed. Or Bethesda . . ."

"Kenny . . ."

"Even a private hospital, I suppose."

"Kenny, tell him no."

"I'll supervise the whole procedure, if you'd like. Take care of all the arrangements."

"I don't know."

"I do have to be honest, Mrs. Kennedy. I believe the procedure should be done at a military hospital. President Kennedy was the commander in chief, so I think it makes the most sense, regarding personnel, security, and clearances. Again, I'm sorry for the frankness. But it is mandatory."

She tries to protest one more time, picturing those stories about how an Indian could rip out your heart so fast that you could still see it beating outside your body, but Dr. Burkley keeps repeating that *it's mandatory, it's mandatory, it's mandatory,* and neither Kenny nor Pam seems willing to contradict this, until she can't stand to hear *it's mandatory* one more time, and finally says, *Okay, then do it at Bethesda,* and before she's finished speaking, she feels like that ripped-out heart, thumping on its own, looking back at a body so alive it doesn't know it's dying.

The Memory of the Lens: Part One.

There is clotted blood on the external ears but otherwise the ears, nares, and mouth are essentially unremarkable. The teeth are in excellent repair and there is some pallor of the oral mucus membrane. (Page 3, Pathological Examination Report, 11/22/63)

It's one of the photos of the autopsy. His head. Photographed from the neck up, with just a trace of his shoulders and chest, enough so that you can tell he's undressed. It's a simple picture, one snapped by the medical photographer John Stringer on a four-by-five Graphic camera. But what's so amazing about the picture is how dead Kennedy looks. And it's not Hollywood dead, with passively closed eyes and a nodded head that suggests the sleep of the just. In the photo, his head is tilted back, eyes wide open, and his mouth ajar, without any sense that he's ever lived. A tracheotomy tube pokes out of his throat, as though his survival had been just a matter of extra air. His teeth look a little bucked. You can stare and stare and stare, noting how the tiles in the floor frame the definition of his collarbone and the tufts of chest hair. There certainly are characteristics of the Kennedy you've come to recognize, but when pressed, you'd have to admit that you've never seen anyone look so dead before.

Of course, there was Dominic's father, a big Italian American you barely knew while in college, who was slightly intimidating in his silence, yet who died suddenly and weakly from a heart attack. You went to the funeral because all of Dominic's friends were going to the funeral. You'd never seen a dead body before. It was an open casket, and it felt as though you stared harder and longer than anyone else, because you couldn't get over how different he looked, his face made up and shaded orange, thinner than normal, as though a lesser artist had crafted him from wax. Within the year you would attend two more funerals, but both with closed caskets. In the case of Susie it was because she'd died from her own shotgun blast in her bedroom, surrounded by notes and disappointments and teddy bears. And in the case of your grandmother it was because of the disfigurement of the auto accident (although they did hold a viewing; but, remembering Dominic's father, you elected not to go, too afraid that the distorted image of the repaired face would become the everlasting memory).

It all makes you think of souls. Though you make no claims to belief, seeing that picture of Kennedy suggests that there must be more to the body than hardwiring and chemical messengers that trick the body into being, because even a piece of machinery stripped of its functioning parts still looks like the machine. Perhaps it's just back to Descartes' *earthen machine*. Or Thomas Aquinas's reconciliation of the *eternal soul* with Aristotle's *intellective soul*. Or maybe it's all just smoke and mirrors, a hypnotist's whisper and suggestion that makes you believe that there's something more than parts and components. Maybe when the body dies, the hypnotist's fingers are snapped, and we stop barking like dogs, and look around, suddenly recognizing the machinery. Maybe we even laugh a little at ourselves.

The complexity of these fractures and the fragments thus produced tax satisfactory verbal description and are better appreciated in photographs and roentgenograms which are prepared. (Page 4, Pathological Examination Report, 11/22/63)

John Stringer is waiting in the morgue for his subject. FBI and Secret Service agents stand around in civilian clothes. The three doctors in charge—Boswell, Humes, and Finck—also are waiting, silent, reorganizing their tools and equipment over and over. Others start to trickle into the room. Dr. Burkley lingers in between, looking uncertain of his responsibility as an observer. One of Stringer's students, Floyd Riebe, leans into the corner of the room, clutching a small 35 mm Canon under his arm. He's here to assist. But mostly it seems as though he'll observe.

A sign is taped to the wall. *Hic locus est ubi mors gaudet succurrere vitae.* "This is the place where death rejoices to help those who live."

Stringer clamps the camera down on the three-wheel tripod. The four-by-five Graphic is heavy as can be. He snaps on the giant flash, thinking this might be the last time he has to use the camera because the commanding officer won't let him buy any more four-by-five film since he's agreed to convert the whole operation to 35 mm.

Morgue lighting is always ridiculous, fluorescents and an operating lamp that won't allow for the most basic exposure. So he has to set up two speed lamps, mounting them on stands with rollers, double-checking the synchronization to make sure they'll flash with the camera. Maybe that will also change with the upgrade.

The casket is wheeled in and then opened. He watches the hinges. The body is wrapped in hospital sheets inside a body bag. Towels are padded around the head. The room smells rotten, slightly tempered by the sterility of the alcohol and rubber gloves. The civilians step forward a little, out of curiosity, but then step back as quickly. Kennedy's eyes are wide open. The doctors shut them. But they pop open again.

Stringer returns to setting up his equipment. Somehow he'd been anticipating something more.

X-rays are taken. The machine sounds like rocks and gravel. A construction site.

After about a half hour, Stringer asks, "Are we ready?" He stands back, loading film from the two-pack into the Graphic.

Dr. Boswell asserts his position as chief of pathology at all times. He says he just wants to make sure the X-rays come back clean, that's all. "Now we can start cutting."

There is surprisingly little reverence in the room. Maybe it's shock, or just old-fashioned professionalism. But it seems that nobody is thinking about this in terms of history.

Stringer lines up the camera and shoots down on the body, trying to capture the full length, from head to toe. He pushes himself back farther and farther, until he has the full perspective in the lens. Somewhat satisfied with the angle, he presses the shutter, and the flash from the speed lamps bursts out, freezing everybody for a moment.

Following the doctors' lead, Stringer starts moving more quickly. Loading up round after round, he hands off the exposed film holders to Riebe or to one of the agents, who drops them in a box earmarked for processing.

He shoots the head. The scalp. Normal. Peeled back. Then the doctors prop Kennedy up, sitting at a ninety-degree angle.

Again, the eyes pop open. A Secret Service agent looks away.

Stringer moves quickly to get the camera in place. Kicking at the lamp rollers. Dragging the tripod. Riebe has retreated to the back of the room. The doctors are looking at Stringer, almost out of breath, hoping he can load the camera quickly, since the body is all weight at this point. He shoots as fast as he can, his only perspective what he sees through the viewfinder. If anybody were to ask him later what he saw, he'd be hard pressed to give an accurate description other than how he remembered the basic composition.

After the body is laid back on the table, Boswell announces that they'll begin the Y incision. Stringer doesn't need directions. He's shot this procedure a hundred times or more over the years. The camera instinctively will follow the pathologist's scalpel, as if it were the doctor's eye. Starting at the chest and then cutting down through the waist. Always clean, with almost no blood. While one doctor is sawing open the chest cavity, removing the breastbone and ribs, the other is examining the abdominal cavity. Major organs are cut out, weighed on a grocer's scale, then set beside a ruler to be photographed before being put in a jar with preservative. They dissect the liver and move on to the lungs, the pancreas, spleen, kidneys, and stomach. And the speed lamps flash for each organ, like a Hollywood premier. Each burst is the only sound in the room.

They examine the scalp. Note every defect caused by the bullet. Sample the bits of matter that have hemorrhaged through the fractures. Then without pause, they saw off the top of the head, remove the brain, and preserve it in a fixative for further examination at a later date. A big sewing needle is pulled out to stitch the skull and the trunk with a seam that will look like the side of a baseball.

There's a collective sigh. Someone says to Stringer, "So you got those all?"

"Of course," he says. He's palming a receipt. The Secret Service has taken possession of the films. They'll handle the developing.

Stringer puts the Graphic away and folds the tripod. Rolling the lights toward him in order to break them down. He glances back at the operating table. Kennedy's eyes have popped open again, and though they are fixed upward, it seems as though they follow him, creepily, like one of those haunted nineteenth-century portraits.

He looks back down at the receipt, focusing on the name, *Kennedy*. A wicked little scrawl that seems too impersonal not to be real. Too real, in fact.

Stringer supposes he could fall apart and cry, collapse, become undone, and blame it on the exhaustion of the day. But instead he continues to break down his equipment. Leaving the wing nuts loosened on the speed lamps. Knowing he'll need to set them all up again in a week or so, when the team reconvenes to finish up with the dissection of the brain.

In addition, it is our opinion that the wound of the skull produced such extensive damage to the brain as to preclude the possibility of the deceased surviving this injury. (Page 6, Pathological Examination Report, 11/22/63)

You look at the picture longer and longer. Wanting to see something. A glimpse. A fraction of something familiar. Maybe if his expression looked a little more shocked. A little more dismayed and terrorized. But he's just so vacant. Eyes staring up dumbly, the pupils dilated, with a dulled, milky film. And you wonder how he could have absorbed so much shock and trauma and come out like this, almost lamely passive. The pathologists maintain that the body is the record. And from a scientific perspective they're probably correct. But in the photograph, he's just a body. It's only memories that will bring him to life.

In the photograph, he just looks so dead.

The Seventeenth Floor.

On the seventeenth floor of the medical towers at the Bethesda Naval Hospital, they are gathered while the autopsy is being conducted in the morgue below. Jackie. Bobby. Close friends. Aides. Family members. The Secret Service has sealed off the floor. Special phone lines have been set up, with both direct communications to the White House and to the morgue.

Jackie is becoming more and more anxious. Disoriented. Like a sleepwalker who's been wakened. Instinctively, she works the room like a hostess. All manners. Automated graces. She appears perfectly natural, as long as her vacant eyes are avoided and her bloodied dress is ignored.

For a moment she pauses to stare out the window. Looking down on the city. It's dark and it's late, but not as late as it looks. A few headlights trickle down the streets, distinct and cutting. She can see houses still lit with television sets. Little ghostly glows radiate from each one. She wishes for nothing more than to be in one of those bungalows, sitting on the couch with dessert on her lap yet too upset to eat, watching the television and pitying the misfortune of someone else's life.

Bobby touches her hand. She startles. "I've just spoken with Dr. Burkley downstairs," he says. "I told him about this procedure. How it's all taking much too long."

"What did he say?"

"He says he can't control the procedure. It's all law. It's mandatory. Imagine. He's telling me about the law."

She whispers back, "I told you." In his eyes she sees total devastation. He looks more broken than she feels, which somehow is logical since she's not feeling much of anything at all, as if her nerves have been surgically removed. Still, seeing him makes her wonder if she's a little less capable of grief.

Bobby shakes his head. "I don't see the point of all this."

"I don't know."

"Maybe I'll just go down there myself. Make them stop this nonsense."

"Maybe you should."

She watches him slip out the door, mumbling something to the military guard. The suite is filled to capacity. Quiet. People speak in whispers. Still, her head is banging, and she wants to put her hands over her ears. Medications don't work. One hundred milligrams of Vistaril shot right into the arm by her own doctor has had no effect. She just might explode, if not for manners.

Ben and Tony Bradlee make their way to her. Tony says she's so sorry, and if there's anything Jackie needs, they are always there. Ben reaches out for Jackie, but hesitates, noticing the caked blood that dots her forearm.

She looks at him, managing to hold her stare for a moment. They were at the White House earlier. She hopes they don't bring up the children. She barely can manage as it is. Even the mention will undo her. She needs to be talking. Taking control. Believing there are no ripples beyond this suite. "Do you want to know what happened?" she asks. "Do you want to know?"

Ben stutters a bit. Looks to Tony. Composes himself in politeness. "Of course," he says. "Of course."

She begins, "It was out of nowhere," but then stops herself. Her tone deepens. If only for a split second, she sounds completely lucid. "This is all off the record. You know that. All off the record."

Ben nods, looking a little hurt. But these things have to be said, even among friends. "I don't know," she begins. "The weather wasn't what anybody expected. And maybe we should've been thinking the worst, but we weren't . . . Excuse me for a moment."

She's barely down Elm Street before the first interruption. Kenny with something from the White House. The Bradlees wait patiently until she picks up the story again. Then it's Larry breaking in about funeral arrangements. McNamara with the burial site. Her aides trying to get her to change her clothes.

A moment before the shots are about to be fired, Bobby comes back into the room and apologizes to the Bradlees. He needs to talk with Jackie. Pulling her to the side, he looks flustered, eyes darting, his hands balled into fists. Although his voice remains steady, he can barely speak. "I don't know what's going on down there," he says. "They're just going and going. It's as though those doctors don't know the difference between a forensic autopsy and a regular hospital pathological autopsy." He uses the medical terms awkwardly, as though he's just learned them.

"You're the attorney general."

"Jackie, they don't care what we have to say."

"Maybe *I* should call, Bobby. Do you think I should call down there?"

"They're not listening."

"I can call."

"No one listens. I've never seen anything so . . ."

They pause. Out of the corner of her eye, she sees the Bradlees still standing, looking unsure if they should wait for her to return with the end of the story. She tries to nod, or to give some gesture that indicates she's finished. It's probably better to keep the story in the middle.

Bobby says he's worried a pathological autopsy will bring up other things. And she asks, "Other things?" and he says, "Yes. You know."

She looks at him quizzically.

"His health. All the medications. We don't need that."

"No, we don't need that."

"People have worked too hard to distort his image as it is, and we certainly don't need to help them. That's what I'm trying to tell those doctors. Especially Burkley. You don't need to go into his glands. Don't need to list all the medications. You just need to understand the patterns of the wounds."

"Maybe I should try, Bobby."

"I'm telling you, they don't listen. They don't care what they reveal."

She doesn't push it, because although she understands the implications, and that there will be handfuls of people poring over the reports in order to find something to tear down Jack's image and reveal him as some kind of weakened poseur, that's really not the most distressing thing. It is the pure and simple fact that three men are dissecting Jack's body. And that he lies prone on a table, fully exposed, his organs being weighed, as bureaucrats make notes about him as though he were a specimen.

"I don't know what to do, Bobby."

"Maybe I'll go down there again."

"I'll go with you."

"That's not a good idea. Believe me."

"There are none."

"None what?"

"Good ideas."

Bobby stops himself. His leg is trembling. He breathes so hard through his nose that it whistles, and though he looks at her when he talks, he can't seem to hold eye contact very long. "I'll call first," he says. With that, his voice buckles, and she can see his words literally swallowed, sickening his stomach. "I'll call," he says. "I'll let you know what I hear from the call."

She looks back again to the Bradlees, but they are now sitting on folding chairs, a little slumped, shaking their heads in conversation with Larry O'Brien. She takes the opportunity to go back to the window and look out over the cityscape.

A wood thrush wings by, alone and oddly confused by the altitude. She watches it circle down toward land, settling on a naked tree, bending the edge of the bough slightly and riding it with the breeze. The bird is motionless but still manages to bounce the tree. And she starts thinking about an obscure fact she'd once read about the Australian apostle bird, so named because it travels in groups of twelve—like the twelve apostles of Christ. This story told of three baby apostle birds that found themselves on the ground for some reason, stunned in helplessness, while the safety of their nest waited about forty feet above them. Then a whole caboodle of grown-up apostle birds surrounded the three babies, pushing at them, trying to get them to fly, encouraging them to get back to the nest. Two of the babies tried and tried, and soon enough they were off and flying. But the third couldn't get it. For three days the group of adults came back, trying to cajole the last baby bird into flying. On the third day, when it must have become clear that the bird just didn't understand or was refusing for some unknown reason, the adults lifted into the air in resigned grace and defeat, and then, in perfect precision, fell in unison on the third baby and killed him.

The Memory of the Lens: Part Two.

Floyd Riebe hadn't heard of John Stringer before studying with him at the Naval Medical School. But once he was there, Floyd learned that Stringer had one of the best reputations in the business as a medical photographer. Floyd, a hospital corpsman, joined Stringer's class in March, and by November he was eager to graduate. He'd already witnessed three or four autopsies, helping out as an assistant. Watching how to set the lighting. To move with the doctors. He liked the precision of the work. The accuracy it commanded. In a matter of months he could strike out on his own. Get rid of those giant four-by-five Graphic cameras that seemed rooted to another era, and rely on the quicker, more modern Canon 35 mm.

On November 22, Floyd was on evening duty when a *Washington Post* reporter called, trying to broker a deal for prints or negatives. "I don't know what you're talking about," Floyd said. "Prints and negatives for what?"

"The autopsy," the reporter replied. "You know it's going to be at Bethesda. I'm just looking for an exclusive. Everybody wants answers. Help me out here."

"Well, this is news to me. But even if . . ."

"It's in the public interest. I'd really appreciate whatever you . . ."

"I'm sorry. I just don't know what to tell you."

Floyd went back to the television, looking for the latest updates. Along with everyone else, he'd been watching the news all day long. That was as close to knowing anything there was to know.

An hour later the chief of the day sent word that everybody should be prepared and on alert. Kennedy's remains were en route to the hospital. Floyd called Stringer, who said he was on the way. Since the hospital would not be letting anybody in or out, Floyd was charged to wait at the front entrance in order to confirm not only that Stringer was who he claimed to be but also that he was needed inside the building.

Floyd was ashamed to admit that he felt pretty excited.

In the crowded morgue, Floyd hid in the corner. He was waiting. His skin buzzing electric. He held on to the Canon. Ran the focus in and out.

After setting up his equipment, Stringer walked back, folded his arms, and leaned against the wall. Asked Floyd how he was doing now that he'd hit the big time. If he was prepared. Ready to witness this. "Strange thing how the events on the TV seemed to be taking place in another world," Stringer said, "yet just like that, we're in that world. Like we've entered into the TV."

"Amazing thing," Floyd said. "Does make you a little jittery."

Stringer leaned in closer, drawing his voice down to a whisper. "You have film in that camera? In the Canon?"

Floyd nodded.

"And extras in your pocket? Because if you don't have extras in your pocket, I want you to run down to the office and load up."

"I've got another roll. Maybe two."

"That's good. Good."

"You want me to shoot alongside you or something?"

Stringer slid over closer. "This is an occasion," he said.

"An occasion?"

"An occasion. You should be shooting the whole room. Documenting it. Re-creating the atmosphere."

"That's not too general?"

"It's just as important, in order to understand the whole story."

"You think so?"

"That's why you became a photographer, isn't it? To document the story, yes? Well, this is history, Mr. Riebe, and you're in the middle of it. With a camera . . . An occasion, Mr. Riebe. An occasion."

Floyd patted the spare roll in his pocket. "You think it's okay? I guess I'm still not sure why I'd bother."

"It's your obligation."

The gurney rolled in, its black wheels wobbling and shaking under the weight of the bronze casket. Nobody talked. A tech named O'Conner unzipped the body bag down the middle, stinking up the place to high heaven. He peeled the plastic back while two other men came around to help.

Seeing Kennedy's body on the table was anticlimactic. Lying there naked and stiff, the towels off his head, the president looked no different than the other bodies Floyd had seen. Pale, stupid expressions. Everyman scars. Clumsy, stiffened postures, with their heads awkwardly cradled in a stainless-steel stirrup. No different than the young man who'd died in the tanker accident earlier in the year. Or the old admiral who keeled over into his cereal bowl. And while this should have come as a relief, Floyd felt disappointed.

Stringer was already at the camera, snapping some photos, rolling the lights, while the doctors made general notes and prepared for the X-rays. He looked back once, nodding for Floyd to get going.

Looking around the room, Floyd made sure no one was paying attention to him. He worked his way three or four steps behind Stringer, who was already circling around the doctors, and took a deep breath. One agent got out of his way, apologizing with a side step. He snapped a couple of pictures in the general direction of the autopsy table, capturing both Stringer and the doctors. It seemed a little vague. With all due respect to his teacher, Floyd preferred the absolute. It seemed like direct shots of the body were the best document. Not the atmosphere. Still, he figured he'd try. Supposedly Stringer was the best.

He was able to get a quick series of Kennedy's body. From the unorthodox angle and positioning, Kennedy looked as though he lay alone in the room, disoriented. Then people started to lean over. Interact with the corpse. The movement began to excite the scene. Create a narrative. Floyd had to admit it was nice being freed from the doctors' procedures. He broke away from Stringer. Turning slightly, he felt the motion of the room around him. As though he were part of a film, rolling from frame to frame. More and more he found himself lost to the lens. Watching the events unfold one shutter click at a time. For once, within the experience while capturing the experience.

There were so many telling expressions. The staid but uncomfortable mien of one of the agents. Dr. Humes's eyebrows wrinkling as he turned to respond to Dr. Burkley. The nurses standing a step behind. The political aides conferring with the doctors. One shot captured Bobby Kennedy's shoulder as he leaned anxiously through the double doors, looking for somebody.

Floyd focused on one particular Secret Service agent, catching the exact moment when he glanced at Kennedy's skull, swallowing, his eyes fixed to the side, wearied, and maybe for the first time heartbroken at his failure to protect. And just as Floyd snapped the picture, the agent glared right at him. Face tightening. Lips pursed. He walked over and grabbed the Canon. Popped open the back as if he'd read the owner's manual and stripped the film out the back, holding it up to the light, as though he enjoyed watching it expose. It ended that quickly.

Floyd Riebe had been trained to be loyal only to facts. And he'd embraced that. Maybe too well. Stringer knew. Understood. Maybe that's why he'd told him to document the occasion. To try to find the artfulness. See beyond the objective eye. But it wasn't his way. Wasn't right. It was only a seduction.

Forget art.

Forget artfulness.

Floyd had confined everything he'd just witnessed to the destroyed film, and without it, how could he know anything? He could only be part of an occasion about which he had no memories.

Pushing himself through the crowd, Floyd backed up into a corner. He looked at Stringer, but the big man didn't notice. He watched over the room, reciting the scene to himself. Lips moving, but not speaking aloud, he narrated the precise details. Cataloging the movements of the doctors. The amount of film cassettes used. The order of things. At some point he knew he'd be asked about the experience, and he knew that on some level he would make a story about it (how could he not?), but he wanted to be sure that the story was accurate, the details precise, and that any discrepancies were technical, not interpretive. He said them over and over to himself, reversing the order when needed, blinking his eyes as though developing and fixing them to his memory, knowing that he'd never take another photo for art's sake, believing the bureaucrat's creed that the details are grounded in the world of absolutes.

The Burial Site.

The word is Boston. But no one thinks much of it. Even if it did make sense, it's only out of convenience. The inner circle is asking around. Straw polls on the seventeenth floor of the Bethesda Naval Hospital. They ask Ben Bradlee. He's an original Bostonian. What does he think of it for the grave site? Of Boston? Brookline, where the family plot is. Maybe Cape Cod. He shrugs and says he doesn't like either. But it's only knee-jerk reacting. How could he have thought about it? Who could be giving this any serious thought right now? At least, who other than those who must?

And does it matter that the lineage was to Martha Washington and not to George? Does it help that George Washington always thought of George Washington Parke Custis as his own, even though he was born to Martha's son from a previous marriage? That Washington adopted the boy when his father died from camp fever during the Battle of Yorktown? That there was so much Washington pride running through that family that George Washington Parke Custis built Arlington House as a tribute to George Washington, the man he considered to be more of a father than a grandfather? Does it matter that George Washington Parke Custis had a daughter named Anna Marie, and she married her cousin Robert E. Lee, and that when her father died she inherited Arlington House, and that she and Lee called it home for thirty years, until 1861, when Lee, loyal to his Virginia roots, traded in his U.S. Army stripes in order to command the Confederate army? Does it matter that on May 13, 1864, William Christman of the Sixty-seventh Pennsylvania Infantry Regiment was the first soldier to be buried on the grounds of Lee's estate, which had already been seized by the government due to back taxes and then made a Union headquarters? Or that by the war's end, the grounds interred upward of sixteen thousand? Does it matter that General Miegs of the Union Army had soldiers buried directly in front of Arlington House, just to disgrace Robert E. Lee and to make sure he never returned to the house? To Anna Marie Custis Lee it mattered. After all, her great-grandparents were George and Martha Washington.

Early in 1963, Paul Fuqua was giving President Kennedy a tour of Arlington National Cemetery. As the official tour guide, Fuqua made reference to Memorial Bridge being a symbolic link between the North and the South. President Kennedy hadn't known that and asked Fuqua to tell him more. Together they stood in an untamed spot as Fuqua explained how the bridge had been perfectly aligned between Arlington House and the Lincoln Memorial. The placement and design had been conscious, meant to be seen as a healing gesture. Kennedy and Fuqua looked down the hillside, almost perfectly centered between the two memorials. The sun was shining, and there was a light breeze that whistled through the leaves, and the valley looked so sadly bucolic, as though unscorched by its history. "This is so beautiful," President Kennedy said. "I could stay here forever."

The issue of the burial site has not been brought up with Jackie yet. But the probability of Arlington is becoming more and more likely. And once this autopsy is finished Bobby is going to look at the site, the space where Jack stood when he said he could stay there forever, and see if it is a place he in fact thinks his brother could stay forever. Then he'll present it to Jackie. They'll need to make a decision. If not by tonight, then by morning, because the area will have to be cleared—apparently the plot is all clay and roots. The more the idea starts to settle, the better it sounds. Plus it's logical. Jack was both a war hero and the commander in chief. He should rest among his peers. And whatever is missing of Brookline or Cape Cod they can bring to him, in memoriam. Cape Cod granite. The fescue and clover of a Massachusetts field. It's all so logical and uncommonly easy. As though they'd been thinking about it for days, planning it out for weeks. Already perfectly natural.

Breaking and Crumbling: Part One.

She asks him if he knows, and Bobby says, "Knows?" and she says, "Yes, do you know what is going on with the procedure? Are they still doing that autopsy?" She's looking right at him, her face stiff and composed, but her eyes drifting elsewhere. It nearly murdered her to say the word.

But there are new pains. They stab in her belly. Deep inside. Shooting up her spine. And they remind her of labor pains. If only she could anticipate them. Yet she can't pinpoint the pains to any particular place or order. Still, when they come she is almost doubled over. Caught between a clenched fist and a scream.

He says, "Let me telephone. I'll check. See what I can find out."

She smiles back at him. "I'm breaking," she says. "I'm breaking all over."

"Breaking?"

"Crumbling. Crumbling apart."

"Should I get Dr. Walsh?"

"He's already tried. I think I might die of an overdose before I feel the effects of his drugs."

"What can I do for you?"

"You can find out. I'm not sure how I'll hold . . . You can find out."

"Right. What they know."

"And when they're going to stop."

"Stop?"

"Cutting him apart."

Fixed in Wax.

Tom Robinson was part of the team from Gawler's Sons Funeral Home that prepared the body for burial following the autopsy. Most of his work began after the arterial embalming. Initially, he assessed the makeup needs for the president. Mostly cosmetic. The facial damage was minimal, just a few marks on the temple, near the hairline. They were small enough that he didn't need stitches to close them. The president's hair could cover the wounds. But, just in case, Robinson would apply a bit of wax to smooth it out. The bigger concern, of course, was the hole in the back of the skull. A piece of rubber was brought in to seal it up. First they had to dry the skin out. Then insert as much of the rubber as they could under the scalp and hair, and then try to sew the skin to the rubber. As Robinson later testified, the objective was to sew it up tight, with perfection and precision. They were afraid of leaks, because "once the body is moved or shaken in the casket and carried up the Capitol steps and opened again, we had to be very careful, there would have been blood on the pillow."

After completing the procedure, Robinson dabbed his sponge along the president's face, evening out his complexion. Brushing his hair in a way that denied any suggestion of trauma.

Breaking and Crumbling: Part Two.

She'll agree to Arlington. And though they'll want the site to be nearly in front of the Lee house, Major General Jack Graham of the Army Corps of Engineers will succeed in working with the family to move the grave site down, to a point just over the military crest, where it will still be in line with Memorial Bridge but distinct from Arlington House. She won't say much to Bobby and McNamara other than to agree and make sure there is ample space. Already she will be planning to have Patrick's remains removed from the Brookline plot, along with their stillborn daughter, Arabella, buried in Newport, and have them both transported to Arlington to be reinterred, resting beside their father. And when she thinks about the dead babies she'll get those shooting pains again, as though those lost children are still trying to kick and push their way out of her. It's almost a full-body contraction. Maybe when they're laid together, and the physicality of it relieves the shock of dying, the pain will hurt a little less. And her body can stop breaking and crumbling.

A CENTENNIAL FUNERAL
(facts & stories)

IN PROCLAMATION 3382, dated January 7, 1960, President Eisenhower called on Americans from all arenas to participate in the observances for the centennial of the Civil War, to be celebrated between 1961 and 1965. Topps trading cards climbed right on board. In 1962, they put out a series of eighty-eight Civil War cards that, along with bubble-gum sticks and reproduced Confederate currency, depicted colorful scenes of Civil War moments with titles such as *Destructive Blow*, *Wall of Corpses*, *The Cannon's Victim*, and *City in Flames*. The final card in the commemorative set, #87, was called *The War Ends* (there was a #88, but it was just the checklist). There wasn't a *Lincoln Gets Murdered* card.

By 1961 President Kennedy had to reorganize the Civil War Centennial Commission. What should have been a proper memorial had become a staging ground in which many of the Southern states advocated the preservation of racial segregation while their northern counterparts commemorated emancipation. But perhaps the real downfall of the original commission was its inability to promote the centennial as nostalgia. It was expected to make a celebration of America's military history, not our cultural history. One hundred years was supposed to be significant, a monumental divider that firmly plunked our past into history. But instead it exposed the ugliness with an almost sanctioned attention, delivering the message that one hundred years is barely enough time for the wound to scar.

In addition to replacing members of the committee, President Kennedy did his part to turn the conversation back to a nostalgic American narrative in which freedom and victory always triumph through moral and physical strength. Speaking to descendents of the Civil War Medal of Honor winners on the South Lawn in April of 1962, he spoke about how the memory of the great Civil War battles "gives me, as an American, a source of satisfaction to realize that we are the inheritors of that great martial tradition . . . I don't think that there is any feat of arms that is more dramatic than the Andrews Raid—and all the actions of the Civil War, the Indian Wars that followed, and the wars in this century."

Now they were getting a handle on it.

A centennial perfectly suited for Topps bubble-gum cards.

— — — — —

Nelson Pierce found out about Dallas at the East Gate of the White House. He'd left his part-time morning job on Fifteenth Street NW at a little past one thirty, heading over the few blocks to the White House, where he'd start his afternoon shift as the usher on duty. As one of five ushers, Nelson's job was to make certain that the first family had everything they needed. A car. A piece of furniture moved. Food. Something for the children. If the White House residence were a hotel, the ushers served as its hotel managers. They hired and oversaw the servants, as well as controlled the entertainment budget. But the true managerial duties rested with the chief usher, Mr. West. Nelson, along with the other three—Scouten, Carter, and Hare—ran the floor.

He got to the East Gate at a quarter to two, about an hour before his shift began. When the family was out of town, he was usually able to leave an hour early, and on a Friday night, after putting in some morning hours elsewhere, that seemed like something of a perk. It's easy to picture him walking up casually. Knowing it should be a relatively quiet day and already thinking about what he might do with the evening's extra hour. He probably would not have recognized the urgency of the policeman at the gate, trying to will him forward, wanting Nelson to move more quickly but not able to move himself. The policeman nearly left his post to get to Nelson. "Pierce," he said, "hurry and get to the office. The boss has been shot."

And it's easy to picture Nelson partially smiling, unsure of what gives, but his mouth slowly dropping open when he realized the policeman wasn't playing. That his expression wasn't breaking. And that the policeman's voice was shaking when he looked at Nelson, and said, "I'm on the level."

Mrs. Kennedy had radioed Mr. West from the airplane. Already she'd given instructions on how the ushers should begin preparations for both the president's return and his funeral. For the ushers it must have been a relief to be given a firm direction, clearly understanding that all their protocol and training and systems were now useless. Still, Mrs. Kennedy's directives were as vague as they were specific. Or, as Nelson Pierce later recalled, the ushers were to look up the "details of the Lincoln funeral so that we could have things as near as possible to the way they were at the time Lincoln was assassinated."

So many people in charge. The president's brother-in-law, Mr. Shriver; Mr. Miller, chief of ceremonies and special events for the Military District of Washington; and the president's assistant, Mr. Dungan. Plus, behind the scenes, there's General Wehle, commander of the Military District of Washington; the attorney general; Mr. West, of course; and people Nelson has never seen before.

In keeping with the Kennedy White House, there is a strange confluence of honoring tradition while keeping an eye trained on the future.

For many, it's a matter of dusting off old books. Following established customs. Where the navy, coast guard, marine, army, and air force bands rehearse the familiar ceremonial scores. And the joint-service cordons are positioned in their proper places. Cannon salutes. Honor guards.

But then there is Mrs. Kennedy.

She understands that, like her White House redecorations, her husband epitomizes the bridge between tradition and progress. She must remember sitting next to him in the Monroe Room before a television audience as he talked about the role of history, reciting from the stone plaque in front of the National Archives that quotes *The Tempest*: "What is past is prologue." He then elaborated, "This country has passed through very difficult days, but it *has* passed through them." And during this Civil War centennial period, it is she who must realize that they really have passed through history. So fast that it maybe has gotten ahead of them. Staring them sadly in the face. And it's from here that she'll now have to take her husband forward, both into that past and beyond it.

It's her composure, Nelson thinks. Still in Air Force One. She is meticulously and logically orchestrating the funeral, when the idea of a funeral must seem equal parts blindsiding and bewildering. He imagines the shock—not only of losing her husband but especially of witnessing the sudden violence that took him. Nevertheless, it's her composure that is holding this scrambling effort together, even amid the clout of all the leaders. And for that, there must be both shame and gratitude.

Mr. West initially informed the ushers that Mrs. Kennedy would be arriving with the president's body at about eleven o'clock that evening. It seems impossible for the funeral preparations to be accomplished by then. The physical work alone will take hours, much less the research, location of materials, coordination of efforts. It's best not to look at the clock. It's best not to watch something passing that one can't slow down. Or just stop.

— — — — —

The catafalque would be the easiest place to start. A basic bier, following Lincoln's shooting it was designed quickly by Benjamin French for the president's casket to rest on while he lay in state, built from just a few rough pine boards, framed and nailed together, and covered with a deep black drapery. It had been used fourteen times since it was built. Stored under glass in the Capitol basement, in the so-called Washington's Tomb, the crypt where George and Martha had planned to be buried. So when the ushers are directed to start assembling the pieces of the Lincoln funeral, arranging for the catafalque seems the easiest place to start. There already is a procedure. One that is understood.

It is a structure in which the materials lack the elegance of Washington pomp. Almost like a stage prop. Strips of ordinary wood hammered by a carpenter's hand but covered in elegant cloth, as if to mask the simplicity and haste. But set up in the East Room, while the ushers decorate and the servants clean and the guards stand waiting for the casket to arrive, there is a sense of life that comes to the catafalque. It becomes more than just an object of significance. More than furniture. And while the tendency may be to admire it, to consider what it has seen and represented, having it placed in the East Room, awaiting the body of President Kennedy, strips it of the nostalgia. It is now part of this world. Severing history. Making us believe that we've made no progress over the past hundred years.

— — — — —

Hours have passed. The White House barely seems any more prepared for receiving President Kennedy's body than it was when they first started. They'll never be ready by eleven. At least Nelson is thinking about that instead of about President Kennedy. Until he thinks that thought.

— — — — —

The White House Library was part of Mrs. Kennedy's 1961 restoration. With the assistance of Jeanette Lenygon, cochair of the American Institute of Interior Designers Committee on Historic Preservation, Mrs. Kennedy turned what had once been a nineteenth-century laundry room into a sitting room that was both elegant enough for entertaining and practical enough to serve an important function as a working library for the president, his family, and his staff. She and Lenygon were able to arrange a donation of the most intact collections of furnishings built by the great New York cabinetmaker Duncan Phyfe. Elegant in deep mahogany, Phyfe's work transformed the library into an early Federalist sanctuary, punctuated by a wood chandelier, gilded in gold, that had once belonged to the family of James Fenimore Cooper. But the books for the library were not just period-piece decorations. In planning for the redecoration, a committee was formed to select titles that would catalog the history of the United States. Over two thousand, either chronicling American history or showcasing important American writers. She knew each book that went on the shelves. What its viewpoint was. What it represented. Why it was shelved. So it makes perfect sense that she would have sent her staff to the library for the books on Lincoln. And maybe somewhere there was a satisfaction in knowing the library was being used. Serving its purpose beyond high teas and meetings.

— — — — —

After a while they're just words. In the library on the ground floor, Nelson reads page after page detailing all aspects of Lincoln's funeral. And he knows he can take notes. Make sketches. Trace the routes. But still, there is no sense of truth to it. They're only stories, and he doesn't imagine Mrs. Kennedy wants to retell a story, but rather capture an essence. Still he searches and searches, and there is no essence. Just clinical accounts. Formal observations. But maybe that is what she wants. Maybe she does want to re-create the set. And it is just a matter of the right fabrics, reviving the caisson. Maybe it's really about obliterating a moment and taking it back to that other place a hundred years ago, when it seemed as though the world had some sense of dignity and the edges weren't so crass. There is still a place for the president there. Even in violence the world seems a little softer, and there already is certainty that his legacy will be one in which tragedy inspires hope.

But Nelson doesn't know.

So in the meantime he'll take notes. Gather procedures. Make lists. Not sure what he's searching for anymore. Just trusting that the meaning is there for her.

They'd worked through dinner, and by eight it seemed as though they'd still barely accomplished anything. They followed the directions of Mr. Shriver. Decorators and artists came and went. Various books arrived showing perspectives of Lincoln's East Room. And at times Nelson again would be sent to the library to find another book, or out front to grab fabric swatches to show Mr. Shriver, or Mr. West, or whoever else would be taking charge. He'd be relaying messages to the servants about which rooms to prepare for which guests. Or up on a ladder, stringing crepe.

— — — — —

Silk crepe is the fabric that most symbolizes mourning. By weaving the silk with small, crosswise ribs, a lightweight and delicate fabric is made, both fragile and strong. As with all mourning materials, it is dyed black, representing the extinguishment of light. But in the nineteenth century, at the time when the East Room was being decorated for Lincoln's body to lie in repose, the fabric was still extremely labile. A light rainstorm would cause the crepe to nearly disintegrate, shriveling it into a barely recognizable version of its once elegant form. In the twentieth century, a waterproof crepe was introduced. A man-made mutation, invented in order to improve the tradition. Turn a past frailty into another nostalgia that romanticizes simplicity, yet honors progress. But even with that, when the rains fell on the improved silk crepe, there was little difference. It still wasn't able to maintain its form.

— — — — —

Mrs. Kennedy wants a riderless horse. She remembers it from the Lincoln funeral. An imperative. Although Nelson knows that's military, a full-honor tradition, there's so much he doesn't know about it. So he's back to the library, thumbing through the books again, trying to gather the protocol, glean the meaning. Learning that although people say it's a riderless horse, in fact the real term is a *caparisoned horse*. And it follows behind the caisson in military funerals reserved for high-ranking officers, with an empty saddle, and its rider's boots faced backward in the stirrups, signifying that its fallen hero will no longer ride. The caparisoned horse was first used for a president in Lincoln's procession, partly based on the idea that he was the commander in chief. It is symbolic of the heroism of the fallen soldier, but in Lincoln's case the lone horse carried a deeper resonance, the slow trot of a nation that so suddenly lost its top commander. As Nelson reads this his chest goes hollow, because already he understands nothing will capture the tragedy of Dallas as much as the sight of that empty saddle on a proudly elegant march down Constitution Avenue.

Nelson calls over to General Wehle's office at the Military District of Washington and relays Mrs. Kennedy's wish to an assistant whose name he can't make out. He uses the proper terms, and it is all abstractly official. The assistant says General Wehle has already been informed of the request, and that the duty will fall to the Third U.S. Infantry Regiment's Caisson Platoon at Fort Myer, where the horses are stabled. Nelson takes notes, asking for confirmation on all the spelling, explaining that although he realizes it's being taken care of, he still wants to have all the information correct for Mr. West, should Mrs. Kennedy ask. Even though the assistant isn't obligated to tell him, he does. Nelson learns that the caparisoned horse will be a Morgan quarter horse named Black Jack. A sixteen-year-old black gelding originally from Oklahoma. The assistant tells him that the term "Morgan" means Black Jack is a direct descendent of the colonial schoolteacher Justin Morgan's first horse, Figure, an eighteenth-century stallion reared in Vermont that was legendary for both his strength and poise. He asks where in Vermont, and the assistant says Randolph, and Nelson writes it down, understanding that it really doesn't matter, but it gives a slight feeling of control to have a handle on all the details in a day that otherwise seems out of control. Then he asks when he came to Fort Myer, and the assistant says, *Justin Morgan?* And Nelson says, *No, no, I mean Black Jack*, and the assistant laughs for a moment and says, *I was going to say. Justin Morgan's been dead since around 1800.* And so Nelson says, *Yes, Black Jack. When did he come to Fort Myer?* There's a pause. And Nelson hears papers shuffling. The assistant says, *Well.* Then he says, *Okay, now. 1953. 1953 he joined the Old Guard at Fort Myer.* Again he pauses, and then says, *Oh my. Well, I'll be. Black Jack came to Fort Myer on November 22. Arrived on November 22, 1953.* And Nelson doesn't say anything, and neither does the assistant.

As it neared eleven, it became clear that they could not finish in time. And though he tried to kick into another gear, Nelson was tired, beat up, and wanted to just fold into himself, defeated. Then Mr. West gathered his ushers together. He had a slight smile. There was a delay at the hospital in Bethesda. The president was not expected back for several more hours, more like 4:00 AM. With that announcement, Nelson remembers, they were happy. He doesn't use the word *relieved.* He states very clearly that he was happy. And it's easy to imagine. Maybe it was a second wind. A loss of sense. But the president's body arrived at the White House at 4:20 AM, with the final piece of crepe hung just ten minutes before. And though they probably didn't share a word when the last tack was hammered, in the intervening ten minutes they surely would have felt pleased with themselves. Glanced around the room in pride, admiring their work. Happy to have had the extra time.

— — — — —

The assassination of Abraham Lincoln gave birth to the modern American state funeral. The scope of his funeral is often attributed to the technical revolution in the form of the telegraph and the railroad networks, shrinking the country in a way that allowed for a much more collective grief. It was a funeral for a king—something the founding fathers had eschewed in their fervent rejection of anything that smacked of the monarchy. As the culmination to the series of firsts that defined Lincoln's presidency, his body lay in state in the Capitol rotunda on the hastily constructed catafalque, while thousands of mourners waited in lines for hours to pay their respects. One imagines how the easy spreading of the news would have heightened the grief. The tragedy being relayed in real time through telegraph offices all over the country. If two generals at Appomattox shaking hands hadn't been the first step toward making the individual states feel like one country again, perhaps Lincoln's death had—for better or worse, a common experience that everybody shared in near real-time.

A fact: Within two hours, 90 percent of Americans had learned about Kennedy's death. It was the true coming out of television, which allowed for an instantaneous dissemination of information but, more important, also allowed for a community of witnesses to grieve and process in common, watching events unfold in their living rooms in New York, yet experiencing the exact same moment as their relatives in Sacramento. It one-upped the telegraph of the Lincoln funeral. And by creating a collective consciousness, the television coverage tangentially created nostalgia in real time, a memory without a future or a past.

GO TO SLEEP

1. Paid Holidays

On November 28, 1963, the *New York Times* will report that
John F. Kennedy's name was removed from "the payroll as
President, effective Friday, Nov. 22, at 2:00 PM Eastern standard time." However, the action was not taken until Tuesday,
November 26, when the General Accounting Office reopened,
after closing on Monday for the official day of mourning. But
also effective Friday, November 22, at 2:00 PM Eastern Standard
Time was when the GAO added (or as the *Times* says, "substi-
tuted") the name of Lyndon B. Johnson. His vice-presidential
salary of $35,000 nearly tripled at that moment. With Monday
being his first paid holiday.

2. *The Phone Call: Part One*

December 2, 1963. President Johnson will be sitting in the White House, kicking his feet up, staring out the window with his back to the door, cradling the telephone in the crook between his shoulder and chin. He'll call her *sweetie*. He'll tell her she's got some things to learn, and that one of them is that she doesn't bother him. He'll say, "You give me strength," and he'll tell her he doesn't want letters from her. "Just come on over and put your arm around me. That's all you do. When you haven't got anything else to do, let's take a walk. Let's walk around the backyard and just let me tell you how much you mean to all of us and how we can carry on if you give us a little strength." And he'll tell her that females have a courage that men don't have, and so everybody is relying on her, that in fact she has the President of the United States relying on her, and he's not her first president, at that. "There're not many women," he'll say, "you know, running around with a good many presidents." And she'll laugh, and turn her voice almost girlish, and reply, "*She ran around with two presidents.* That's what they'll say about me."

Maybe that will be the point when she knows she's never going back?

3. *The Politics of Grief (some facts)*

A memo from Assistant Attorney General Norbert Schlei to Pierre Salinger, Johnson's press secretary, dated November 26, 1963, will show the men trying to work out the rights of Jackie Kennedy. There is very little precedent for what is owed to a first lady in this situation, other than to note that there is some precedent for franking privileges for the widows of former presidents, but not by legislation, only by "private acts." Even if there is that entitlement for paid postage, Schlei is quick to point out, "It should be noted that the franking privilege is limited to domestic mail."

There are questions about office space and staff, as though there is a general reluctance to relieve her into civilian life. It seems they're not quite ready to let her go. Schlei rationalizes that because Jackie will undoubtedly be sent untold letters of condolence, and because they will be sent to her as the president's widow, not as a private citizen, the "task of answering this correspondence is a continuation of her duties as First Lady." In light of that, Scheli believes it makes sense that Jackie officially be given office space, supplies, and staff on a limited basis to perform "this last official function." There is no indication of how long that limited period will last. At what point they expect the letters will stop coming. Or that she will stop answering.

Congress will appropriate $50,000 for Jackie to maintain an office over the following twelve months. However, after inventorying staff salaries, materials, and other related costs, the anticipated operating costs come closer to $120,000. In a Christmas Eve memo to Kenny O'Donnell, Bernard Boutin, administrator for the General Services Administration, writes that there are "several alternatives as to how we can handle this." They range from having GSA allocate supplemental monies from its budget, to Mrs. Kennedy paying the difference, to putting a supplemental appropriation before Congress. But they need to exercise caution. The last thing he wants to have happen, Boutin writes, "is to have anything connected with Mrs. Kennedy open to criticism."

On November 29, 1963, George Harris, chief judge of the San Francisco District Court, will write President Johnson on behalf of his court to suggest not only that Jackie continue her role in preserving and refurbishing the White House but also that she be given official status. He suggests that the recognition might help assuage the sorrow of this "symbol of American woman- hood at its best." President Johnson responds by saying that he will do everything he can to "accord suitable recognition to this great lady."

Mrs. D. Jean Mills will write President Johnson a handwritten letter from Middletown, Connecticut, urging a "special medal" for Mrs. Kennedy.

Based on Jackie's "high diplomatic skills, linguistic proficiency, good Catholicism . . . appreciation of art and culture, both past and contemporary," Betty Horne, assistant professor of Spanish at Morris Brown College, will suggest that President Johnson make Jackie his ambassador to Mexico.

When Jackie moves from the White House, two navy stewards will be assigned to help her transition into private life. Because it appears as though it will be an ongoing task, writes Captain Tazewell Shepard in a January memo to the attorney general, her situation becomes unique, not the normal one "to which the restrictions on military personnel performing a job out- side of military service were meant to apply." As naval aide to the president, Shepard, who had been in Dallas, believes that Jackie should still be awarded the stewards, but is concerned for the president's political reputation. "As long as it appears to be an act of moral consideration on the part of the president, it is not likely to become a political issue," he'll write to the attorney general. "However, after what might be considered a reasonable period, it will probably be considered fair political game." He'll suggest some ways to ensure that Jackie can receive the navy stewards, including charging her, including it in the $50,000 appropriation, or assigning retired personnel. He'll save his most radical solution for last—"to have the GAO classify Mrs. Kennedy as a 'Government agency.'"

4. Moving Day (a story)

When Jackie arrives at her new but temporary residence in Georgetown, she'll have been preceded by four days of moving trucks going in and out of the White House, mostly in the rain, dollies bumping across the cobblestones while the movers' hands steadied their loads, looking almost regretful about their task. Most of the items have gone into storage until she finds a permanent home. But on this morning, boxes arrive at the brownstone known as the Harriman House, named for its owner, Undersecretary of State Averill Harriman. The load seems oddly appropriate, almost a reporter's inventory of the Kennedy mystique. Boxes labeled with John's toys, and children's bicycles, and boxes of French wine, and hatboxes, and birdcages, and armloads of White House guidebooks.

It's sunny out. It really should be raining, because that's what the day deserves. And in a black limousine she'll leave the White House with the children. Solemnly, and without expression, following a day of honors and medals, spending part of the morning at the Treasury Department building, watching Clint Hill get the Secret Service Medal for Exceptional Bravery. And maybe he did deserve it; who can say? He did react quickly, running up to the back of the limousine and taking her hand as they fell into the back, and if he hadn't been saving her from the bullets, he surely saved her from flying off the back of the car as it sped away. Then back at the White House she will have said her goodbyes, looking far more comfortable with the staff than with the officials, posing for photographs with each usher in the West Hall, not quite smiling and gazing past the camera, but still withholding the devastation that must have made her wish she had flown off the back of the car.

And it's not more than a ten-minute drive over to the Harriman House on N Street, even less if the driver can avoid the traffic at the intersection of Virginia and Twenty-fifth, but it's a final drive, and the children are in the backseat along with Bobby and Ethel, and the windows are rolled all the way up, tinted, almost ensuring no one could ever find them in the car, and she slumps a little, keeping her head down, vulnerable and ready to scramble away at the slightest disturbance. None of them converse, just rub their hands against their legs, polite smiles when they catch each other's eyes. And it's kind of Bobby and Ethel to come along, though not really necessary, because the truth of it is that leaving the White House was easy—a lot easier than staying there. Already, just minutes past the gates, she can close her eyes and see it as a memory, no longer a reminder. At least in the memory she knows her place there.

About halfway to Georgetown, she brings up one of the letters she received. She's not talking to anyone in particular, and her stare is placed between her in-laws, as though she might be surprised to find out she was talking out loud, that it wasn't just thoughts. There are at least three hundred thousand letters stacked in piles in the East Wing. She's barely looked at any, only the VIPs that her staff felt she should see in order to prepare responses. But every once in a while she opens one of the strays, mostly Mass cards or a specific memory of the president. And she doesn't know if this particular letter stuck out because it was the most recent one she'd read, or because it had some value. It was sent from a woman in Dallas, Texas, who was on the street when the shots were fired, and now she can hardly go to Main Street anymore. Jackie tells them, "She just wanted me and the children to know that Dallas is mourning too . . . And she even included a picture *taken of some of the flowers at the fatal spot.*" Bobby and Ethel don't reply, they just nod their heads. What's eating at Jackie is this strange presumption of connection. She looks at her in-laws. "She sent me a picture of where my husband was shot. You don't think that's . . . ?" and she stops talking because she kind of feels like laughing right now, thinking about this. A picture of where her husband was shot to make her feel better?

As they pull up to the corner, there are photographers standing across the street. The cameras rattle off like typewriter keys as soon as she opens the door, and someone in the entourage says, *For the love of.* And Jackie gets out with the children in tow, with Bobby and Ethel behind them, and they walk up the steps, not really talking until they get to the top, where they confer briefly. It seems so private, despite the cameras snapping, and a little voyeuristic since they appear to have no awareness of anybody around them. There's a boy on a bicycle, riding one-handed, eating an ice cream cone, and he passes in front of the camera, and someone yells at him to get the hell out of the way, while Jackie is shaking her head at Ethel, and then nodding to Bobby, and the two of them turn around and head toward the limousine with the engine still running, and the driver jumps out to get the doors, barely missing an oncoming car, which startles the crowd and the navy stewards, who collectively gasp, then sigh, while Jackie stands on the steps, looking down, holding her keys in her hand, ready to enter her new home with a frightened smile on her face.

A block away, it would just seem to be another black car in Georgetown dropping someone off at midday, the sun raining down over the street and its shoppers and students and businessmen rushing back late from lunch, and one might note how unusually sunny and warm it is for December, and then think to oneself that that means it may be an especially harsh January and February, that we always seem to pay the price for a pleasant day in winter.

5. *The Phone Call: Part Two*

Maybe the December 7 phone call with President Johnson just after she moves to the Harriman House will be the point when she absolutely knows she's never going back?

LBJ: Your picture was gorgeous. Now you had that chin up and that chest out and you looked so pretty marching in the front page of the *New York Daily News* today, and I think they had the same picture in Washington. Little John-John and Caroline, they were wonderful, too. Have you seen the *Daily News*? The *New York Daily News*?

JACKIE: No, but I haven't seen anything today except the *Post* because I just sort of collapsed, but they're all downstairs.

LBJ: Well, you look at the *New York Daily News*. I'm looking at it now, and I just came, sat at my desk, and started signing a lot of long things, and I decided I wanted to flirt with you a little bit.

JACKIE: How sweet! Will you sleep in the White House tonight?

LBJ: [laughs] I guess so. I'm paid to.

JACKIE: Oh! . . . You all three sleep in the same room, because it's the worst time, your first night.

LBJ: Darling, you know what I said to the Congress—I'd give anything in the world if I wasn't here today. [laughs]

JACKIE: Well, listen, oh, it's going to be funny because the rooms are all so big. You'll all get lost, but anyway . . .

LBJ: You going to come back and see me?

JACKIE: [chuckles]

LBJ: Hmm?

JACKIE: Someday I will.

LBJ: Someday?

JACKIE: But anyway, take a big sleeping pill.

LBJ: Aren't you going to bring . . . You know what they do with me, they just keep my . . . They're just like taking a hypo . . . They just stimulate me, and I just get every idea out of every head in my life comes back and I start thinking new things and new roads to conquer.

JACKIE: Yeah? Great.

LBJ: So I can't. Sleeping pill won't put me to sleep. It just wakes me up.

JACKIE: Oh.

LBJ: But if I know that you are going to come back to see me some morning when you are bringing your . . .

JACKIE: I will.

LBJ: . . . kid to school, and first time you do, please come and walk, and let me walk down to the seesaw with you like old times.

JACKIE: I will, Mr. President.

LBJ: Okay. Give Caroline and John-John a hug for me.

JACKIE: I will.

LBJ: Tell them I'd like to be their daddy!

6. Casals's Note (a story)

A note from Pablo Casals's cello floats away through the East Room on a fall evening in 1961. It's the end of the Mendelssohn piano trio, a piece that might almost feel uplifting through its lilting rhythms were it not for the minor key. Although pianist Mieczyskaw Horszowksi and violinist Alexander Schneider both play the final triumphant note, it is Casals whose tone carries throughout the room, resting on a low D. He's stopped bowing, and the piano has stopped vibrating, and the audience is holding its breath before the applause.

Casals's note still hangs.

A rich vibrato, almost honey-toned. No longer aural. It's sensual. Melting on the body, massaging the brain.

Nobody wants to clap. Let out a breath. They want to hold this as long as possible. They could die in it without knowing.

Once the applause begins, she'll smile. Rise from her seat, her beaded silk gown touching the wood floors. Looking around this great room. At the gold curtains and recently marbleized mantels. With the portrait of Washington watching, his hand outstretched and welcoming. The beginning of the restoration. This odd period piece of a house and government center that she has resuscitated through culture and sophistication. As the applause continues to build, she'll swear she sees Casals's note dissipate along the ceiling, watching it undulate and disappear on its way toward the walls. And it will remind her of the impermanence of things. How even in this great moment, her heart will break a little. Looking at the master while he bows with his tuxedo tails flapping against his back. Glancing at Jack. Confirming the joy of her main guest, the governor of Puerto Rico. At only thirty-two, she understands the sadness of experiencing a great moment, knowing that it's already passing even while it's fully alive.

She watches the note slowly disappear into the wall, a last vibration haunting the beams and construction. And she imagines it will stay there forever, becoming part of the White House. Because inevitably someone else will move in and assume that she got it all wrong, or harbor grudges against Jack, or taste, and redecorate the whole building again. But they won't be able to strip the White House of the soul she has built into it. They won't be able to strip it of Casals's last note.

7. The Phone Call: Part Three

In the first week of January 1964, Jackie and President Johnson will talk again by phone. His legs won't be kicked up on the desk this time. He'll be leaning forward on his elbow, resting his head against the receiver. His voice will be lower than normal, like he's tired, but still managing the banter. In only two and a half months, it will be clear how disconnected she is from the goings-on of the White House. And though she'll appreciate his efforts to make her feel as though she still has a place, throughout the conversation it will become obvious that she no longer has that connection. Already she knows she won't last the year in Washington; in fact she can't imagine ever wanting to be there again. The house in Virginia where she and Jack planned to retire will have to be sold. New York is the only place she'll imagine being. Lost in the anonymity of its density.

All this knowledge will be revealing itself while she talks to President Johnson. But still she'll engage with him. A construct of manners. The deaf nod. He's recently given his first State of the Union address, and he complains of being tired. She'll tell him to rest. Take a nap. Take one after lunch, she says. *It changed Jack's whole life.* She tells him that Jack did it every day, just like Churchill. Even if he couldn't sleep, Jack still stopped for the routine of the nap.

LBJ: I'll start it the day you come down here to see me, and if you don't, I'm going to come out there to see you.

JACKIE: Oh, Mr. President . . .

LBJ: And I will just have all those motorcycle cops around your house, and it will cause you all kinds of trouble, and . . .

JACKIE: I can't come down there. I wanted to tell you. I've really gotten a hold of myself. You know, I would do anything for you. I'll talk to you on the phone. I'm so scared I'll start to cry again.

LBJ: Oh, you never cried, honey. I never saw anyone as brave as you.

JACKIE: But I . . . You know . . .

LBJ: Or as great.

JACKIE: I just can't.

LBJ: You know how great we think you are?

JACKIE: Well, you know. I'll talk to you. I'll do anything I can. But don't make me come down there again.

LBJ: Well, I've got to see you before long. I've got to see you.

GO TO SLEEP

Haunting the Lincoln Room: A Story

It's easy to believe in ghosts. Even believe you'd want to become one. How to live together and to die together has never really made sense.

Eternal reunions. Realizing the soul. Rewards for piety and sanctity. Maybe she'll come to embrace at least one of those when she's laid out on her deathbed. But, no, for now she still likes it here. And contrary to the obvious, she doesn't blame the sins of this world for what has happened. Even with Patrick's death. Platitudes about faith and calling mean nothing when you're rushed off to an air force base hospital nearly six weeks before the due date, and they're cutting open your belly, and you're feeling the blood from your uterus trickle down your hips, and everybody in the room is quiet, even the baby isn't crying, and for a moment it occurs to you that you might have died, yet you're not looking down on the room from a white light like the books claim you will; and you hear the doctors talking, and they say they need to airlift the baby to Boston, so you roll your head a little to the side to catch a glimpse of the boy, and your first thought is: Do they make coffins that small?

God took one in the side that day. But it was the rifle in Dallas that finished him off. Lined him up perfectly in the scope this time.

White House history is filled with ghost stories. Spirits that bump and squeak, play with the lights, and slam the doors. A British soldier from the War of 1812 supposedly keeps residence, wandering the grounds where he died, navigating his way with a torch in hand. Mary Todd Lincoln learned words no lady should ever know when she encountered a bitterly muttering Andrew Jackson in the hallway. And there's always a story about the Lincoln Room. Always a longtime staffer who has felt something while passing by the bedroom. Sometimes flitting. Sometimes graceful. And as opposed to the mischievous ghosts who rattle their way throughout the second floor, darting in and out of the Queen's Bedroom, the Lincoln ghost is reputed to be calm, almost welcoming. In his gray pinstripe suit and three-button white spats. Legs crossed, staring straight ahead. But he will disappear on you. Curious and grateful for the company.

You'll never find Jack's ghost here. Make no mistake: he loved the White House and all it represented. But for him it was his office, the tangible symbol of his ambitions. Both he and Jackie had both always been about the moment. But through her work on refurbishing the White House, Jackie had become part of its history. Nailed into the support beams.

In the hallway she runs her fingers along the fabric wallpaper. The staff had been kind enough to wait up for her. They'd all been there, looking down as she passed by. No older and no younger than they were two days ago. And for just a moment she had almost believed the shooting was a wicked figment of her imagination, until she glanced up and saw Miss Shaw. Then she just kept on.

On Valentine's Day, the year before her husband is shot, Jackie gives a tour of the recently redecorated White House to fifty-six million people. The restoration has been her pride, and what had been touted as sort of a ladylike occupation with furnishing and style turns out to be an executive's endeavor of fundraising, historical preservation, and curation, no different than what any major museum might undertake. Escorted by CBS correspondent Charles Collingwood, she almost floats between rooms—her pride, schoolgirl giddiness, and whispery teenage voice at odds with the formal postures refined at Miss Porter's School. But although aesthetics stand as the central theme, it is Jackie's sense of authority that rings loudest. She becomes more than an effete woman leading her audience on a behind-closed-doors house tour; she becomes its link to history. Even when the president makes a cameo at the end, so quickly reducing her to the expected subservience (her body even appears to shrink), it is still Jackie who talks about the history in detail, while the president delivers eloquent but hollow platitudes about learning from history in order to move forward.

Just before they enter the Lincoln Room, the live shot cuts away to a prerecorded spot where she tells us, *Here is what the White House did to President Lincoln . . . This is how he changed.* Slowly she slides us through a series of portraits of Lincoln. *1861* is all she says, and we see a stern but hopeful Lincoln. *1863. 1864.* Even rehearsed and filmed in advance, there is shock in her voice when she says, *1865,* revealing a chiseled half-smiling Lincoln, somehow looking ten times his age. *Just one week before his assassination,* she says. Then pauses, almost as though catching her breath.

She passes by Caroline's room. Puts a hand on the doorknob. Then continues.

She's willing to believe the Lincoln ghost stories. Mr. Pierce says that although he's never seen the ghost himself, there've been more staff sightings than he can count. He's told Jackie that the circumstance is always the same. A janitor. A butler. Or a maid. They come up to him, looking pale and sick, looking around like a secret's on their lips, and he always knows what they're going to report. What they're going to confide. *And do they all report the same thing, Mr. Pierce?* she asked. *Do they always see the same thing?* And he smiled back at her, and told her he always heard the exact same description, from the pinstripe suit to the white spats. She said, *The exact same?* And he said, *The exact same.* That made her laugh, and Mr. Pierce laughed too. *White spats?* she said. They'd laughed together.

The door to the Lincoln Room is open. And she steps forward, almost assessing the potential. Here is the room where he signed the Emancipation Proclamation. The table with Victorian carvings that holds an original copy of the Gettysburg Address. She's always loved the room. The light. The magnolia out the window. And as she steps in farther, she can feel the connection tighten. She wants to lie down on the bed. She'd be willing to die there.

She stares at the carpet patterns and keeps her hands at her sides, fiddling with her fingernails. She can barely see for all her exhaustion, and she's not sure what comes next. She'd be able to handle a chill from Lincoln flitting off the nape of her neck or blowing against her ankles. But not seeing him. She holds her breath. He could be sitting there, watching her. Sitting in that chair, with his legs crossed and his gaze cast forward. Sensing her defenselessness. If things were to go wrong she could always sneak up on him with that same reckless daring of John Wilkes Booth, draw her thumb and forefinger into a gun, pull an imaginary trigger, and say, *Pow*.

The centerpiece of the Lincoln Room is the bed. Measuring six feet by eight feet, the carved rosewood back rises like a lancet arch against the wall. It is both simple and elegant. Bought by Mary Todd Lincoln during her White House restoration, the bed was originally placed in the state guest room. Lincoln never slept in the bed. His eleven-year-old son, Willie Lincoln, did die on its horsehair mattress. And three years later Lincoln was autopsied on a cold table at its foot. It's hard to imagine Mary Todd Lincoln having any reverence for the bed. It's a wonder she didn't take it out back, grab an ax, and chop away at it until it was nothing but splinters and hairs.

Moving toward the bed, Jackie keeps an eye on the empty chair, looking for the white spats. She really just wants to lie down. Just close her eyes for a little bit. But staying awake means she won't have to wake up to this tomorrow. That has to be the harder thing, to already have one day behind you, already beginning to form a new history. Better to live forever in one day. That she understands.

There'd been stories that Jack used the Lincoln bed for some of his affairs. It seems possible enough. Probably true. She had. Kind of. A designer visiting the White House while Jack was away. To discuss the refurbishing. They talked well into the night, sharing a bottle of wine. She'd toured him a little around the White House, talking about the renovations, about the state of literature, but strangely enough never mentioning Jack or the children, nor asking about the source of his wedding band that he kept slightly hidden, often under his right hand. They walked a little closer together. He held doors for her. She laughed at his jokes, which weren't really that funny. She'd entered a life without history. Every minute was regenerating itself, framed by nostalgic décor.

The romantic's belief is that the ideal person already exists somewhere in the world, while the tragedist delights in knowing how rarely they find each other. But here he was. Tall and slightly stooped, leisurely and disheveled despite an attempt at formality, willing to share of himself, but so selectively that she could discern the pattern. And she knew she intimidated him. On the surface this all seemed so impossible. So unlikely.

Climbing the stairs, she'd looked at the designer and felt overwhelmingly sad. It was not so much the schoolgirl feeling of unrequited love that bothered her, but the fact that the very sequence of decisions that had led her to him was the exact same sequence that would make it impossible to be with him.

They walked into the Lincoln Room with intimate and cunning banter. After reciting the highlights, she told him to go look at the Gettysburg Address. He walked back to her side and didn't say anything. Silently, and somewhat surprising to herself, she reached down and held his hand. They made small talk about the history of the room, but she couldn't think about anything other than how much of herself she had just given over, and that that was enough. Somewhat awkwardly, he dropped her hand, not like he didn't want to hold it, but in a way that suggested he was afraid. It was late, he said, and he had to get back to his hotel. As they started to leave the room, she took his hand again and said, *Please*, but then let go. And she said, *I'm sorry*, and he nodded it was okay, and she said, *I hope you don't think*, and he said, *No, it's okay*. But what she couldn't tell him was that she was trying to right every decision she'd ever made in her life with that gesture. And that his touch had the power to undo a life spent trying to give up everything she had, before she'd had it. She wiped her hand along her skirt. Taking his hand had been more daring than anything Jack could have ever done in that room. And so much more damaging.

She's not crazy. It's just crazy behavior. It will probably always be so. It's just a matter of management.

She considers whispering President Lincoln's name. Maybe ask if he doesn't mind if she lies on the bed. Shares the room. And she wonders what she'd say if he answered. She'd be tempted to ask him, *Why?* He might be coy and say he doesn't understand. But she'd work up the nerve and press him a little bit, until he'd finally say, *You mean why stay in the room? Haunting the room?* And she'd say, *Yes, yes,* but immediately recant, and explain that she doesn't want him to answer. Because she knows. Understands. How they've both been damaged by God. How both have been counseled by heaven. And how they both have held their own dead children in their arms. Both known that you don't need to die to be a ghost.

But she just wants to lie down on the bed. The one he never slept in. In this room. Where the series of events is understood. And where it's okay to confess that God has been murdered.

Somehow that seems more daring than dying. Or living.

CODA: Cleaning Up

Here's a final story:

Vaughn Ferguson didn't feel like moving that morning. At barely fifty-three years old, he felt as though he'd aged an extra decade overnight. For more than ten years he had been working in conjunction with the White House garage, serving as Ford Motor Company's liaison to the army's White House transportation agency. He'd come to the post with close to a quarter century's experience as a mechanic under his belt, charged with keeping Truman's Lincoln Cosmopolitan in top order, following the lease agreement between his employer and the Secret Service. Being the man in the middle, Vaughn facilitated a clear line of communication. He took his service seriously, seeing the patriotism in his work, often traveling with the presidents he served, ensuring safe and reliable transportation from a mechanical point of view. And every time he went down to the garage, it felt like an honor to him, still as exciting as the first morning he had entered the official garage at Twenty-second and M. But on November 24, a day that might have been cloudier and colder, Vaughn picked at his wardrobe slowly, trying to find reasons to delay going in.

He knew Maggie was trying to stay out of his way. Neither had slept the night. This morning she'd offered him breakfast. They both knew he'd refuse. She'd been so teary-eyed each time she looked at him that Vaughn had to look away because he knew if he stared too long, he'd break down; and if he broke down now, he'd never be able to report in today with any degree of professionalism. "You'd better go," he heard Maggie say.

Vaughn turned around, still in his blue boxers, holding a pair of gray slacks in his hand. They tilted toward the end of the hanger, bunched up. "I know," he said. "I know."

Maggie said, "You know there's nothing you could've done. You know that, right?" She cinched her robe together.

It was the first she'd said of it directly, and it was that directness that stopped Vaughn, closing off his thinking just enough to scramble his words. "It's not that I ever thought—" he began, and then he stopped.

"Wasn't anything but a rifle," she said. Strikingly composed. "Wasn't anything you could've fixed on that car to make a difference."

"If I'd been there . . . Maybe the bubbletop."

"Was it faulted, the bubbletop?"

Vaughn shook his head. It had never even left the trunk.

"There wasn't anything you could have done. It had nothing to do with the car. You hear me? It had nothing to do with the car."

Vaughn looked at her, avoiding her eyes. In twenty-five years of marriage he'd never seen her so sure of something. It was disarming and confirming. Her hands were steady, straight at her sides near her hips, and it didn't seem to be acting, but pure assuredness. He pulled at the hair on his arm, feeling some shame for causing his wife to have to shoulder the burden. But maybe when it came down to it, Maggie was the one who really carried them. Somewhere along the line they'd just agreed to pretend it was his role.

"All right now," Maggie said. "Time to put on those slacks of yours." She breathed in so deeply he swore he heard her lungs expand. "You're needed by the White House, Mr. Ferguson. Now if you'll excuse me . . ."

He watched Maggie leave the bedroom, then heard the bathroom door shut. Even with her running the hot and cold faucets at full volume, Vaughn could hear her cries. Hard and low, in steady rhythm.

He pulled his pants on, knotted his tie. He didn't check himself in the mirror. Moving quickly, he walked past the bathroom. He'd make sure to slam the front door hard. Then Maggie would know it was okay to turn off the faucets.

It was the red rose petals spread along the rear mouton mat that stunned him. They still held full and colorful. Disconnected from everything, tumbled out of arrangement. And it was strange that anybody would overlook them. Gather evidence, note and catalog everything of importance, yet still leave the petals in the car.

He'd seen the car the day before at the behest of Special Agent Geis. When Vaughn arrived, he'd stood at the entrance to the White House garage, working up the nerve to go in. A crosstown wind chilled his neck. He wiggled his fingers and then scratched at his thighs. Maybe this was what it was like for people called down to the morgue to identify a body. Delaying and pacing. Making yourself believe that once you go in, the mistake will be clear, and the relief will almost make you laugh in a way that isn't funny. Yet deep down, once inside, you know exactly what you'll see.

Geis wasn't there, and Vaughn found himself stymied by the agents guarding the car. Their orders gave him access only to the windshield, with a directive to have it replaced and the damaged one processed as evidence. He stood before the limousine, which was covered sloppily by a canvas tarp. He recognized the Lincoln's contours poking through, especially the curvature of the spare tire. The outlines of the Secret Service's sideboards edged out along the bottom, and, above, the ribcaged ridges framed the bubbletop. A fraction of the tire was caked with mud, dust, and grease. But more than being dirty, it looked worn. Almost as though there were no tread. He wanted to imagine the limousine complete under there, as pristine as the day he had sent it off to Dallas; almost believing that yanking off the canvas would reveal a car unharmed.

He lifted the tarp off the hood and over the windshield. A foul odor of chemicals and old meat rushed out at him. He squinted his eyes and bit down on the top of his tongue, nearly drawing blood.

He had tried to look at the window clinically, knowing he ought to put in a call to the Arlington Glass Company for the replacement. Following along the edges, he avoided the middle, trying not to be hypnotized by the spiderweb cracks that broke out of a single hole near the rearview mirror. What was he supposed to do? No manuals in hand, not even a sense of procedure. He glanced at that little hole near the mirror. Splintered rivers in all directions. He almost gagged.

"If you saw the car," he said to Maggie later in the evening. He sat in his lounger, with the television set on. His eyes drifted over it, fixed on a small crack in the plaster. All evening long that box had been droning, a slow dirge. Although it felt like it was beating him down with its constant reminders, Vaughn had not been able to turn it off. He pictured himself staring at the Lincoln, standing in the shadow of the parking lot, the fluorescents washing out his profile. It had seemed infallible to him. "You've never done anything but the right thing." Maggie was running out of things to say. But it wasn't that her convincing was limited—that much he knew about her; it was that Maggie was finding it difficult to stay positive for her husband. He could hear it in the way she breathed, low and quick, as though the only breath left came from her gut. And he'd felt bad, because all the world was grieving together—through their TV sets and telephones and porch steps and radios and lunchrooms—but Maggie was stuck trying to raise her husband's spirits, talk him into believing that he wasn't the one who pulled the trigger. "It might have been worse if you didn't care for that car the way you did," she'd said, and as she'd said it they both knew that was about all she had left to say. "If you'd seen the Lincoln," he had said. "It just makes you wish you could make it right, is all. Just makes you wish you could make it right." And they had both known that was all he had left to say.

When he entered the garage, Vaughn had heard a slow, steady tapping. It wasn't clear where it came from. He found himself following the rhythmic sound. At times he'd turn the corner, expecting to see the source. Not only would there be nothing there, but the percussion would suddenly seem to originate from the other end of the garage. He felt as though he'd walked three circles around the warren of stalls. Nearing the entrance, he stopped. He started walking again and then suddenly stopped. He drew in a breath, keeping his body so still he thought he might have stopped his heart. There he listened. Listened. The percussive tapping had been from his own feet.

Vaughn knew the FBI had been combing through the limousine for most of the day before. Along with guidance from the White House physician, FBI investigators had gathered up blood and brain matter (brain matter!), bullet fragments from the cushions, journaled the contents of the car (the lap robes in the back, the contents of the trunk), followed up with detailed photographs to support their notes. Vaughn had not exactly been cleared to go over the car. It was more that nobody seemed to care anymore.

The seats had already been given a cursory cleaning, with discolored sponge streaks going against the grain of the leather. At least the Secret Service had tried, but it seemed as though they had just brushed off the seats.

Vaughn opened the rear left door, Mrs. Kennedy's side, and scooted along the leather interior. He reached down to the floor for each petal, gathering them into a single pile, not sure what he would do with them when he was finished. Even if it were just a matter of throwing them away, those rose petals deserved better than being left behind as mop-up from the crime scene.

With the final petal out from under the middle seats, Vaughn scooped them all up with his bare palms. He placed the mound on the garage floor, for some reason compelled to lay them perfectly along the painted yellow line. When he glanced back at the floor mat where his pile had just been, Vaughn noticed a large blood stain matting the mouton. And as he looked at it, he began to smell it. And as he began to smell it, he saw it materialize into some kind of otherly reminder. It became too much to bear, so he pulled out a handkerchief from his pocket and spit into it three times, pushing the kerchief onto the stain before the spit dried. He checked it. The handkerchief was still white. He dabbed a little harder. Still nothing came up. He spit into the handkerchief two more times and scrubbed the stain, thinking he'd develop his own chemical tonight if need be. Anything to lift that stain off the floor.

Splayed out along the backseat, his whole body leaked sweat. He was trying to catch his breath. Beside him, Vaughn noticed an upholstery button ringed by dried blood. A thin, ridged mound, brown and caked, that seeped below the button itself. He backed himself out of the car, taking out a pocketknife from his trousers. On his knees, leaning into the car, Vaughn saw that all the buttons he'd been sitting on were also soiled by blood.

He reached back with his free hand to dust off his bottom.

He leaned back into the interior, pulling his cuff over his left hand as a glove, and lifted up the first button slightly, not wanting to tear the threads. He slowly slid the blade between the button and the seat, scraping back and forth, using just enough of the steel to reflect some light, and moving in quick flits, watching the residue turn to dust. His stomach growled with each swipe.

He spent over an hour working on those buttons. Cleaning all three and then coming back to the first again. Over and over. Not willing to stop until he'd cleaned them beyond a trace. At one point he thought he might have scratched the leather, even sliced it, and he caught his breath, and it held, trapped in his chest. He wasn't sure he'd ever be able to breathe again until he looked closer and saw it was just a surface scratch, easily polished out with spit or solution. And when he scraped up the last of what he could find, Vaughn tried to stand on his pins-and-needles legs, which had lost feeling from being cramped so long. He grasped at the car door when his legs forgot how to support him.

Limping through the garage on his way out, his right leg still dragged a little, not fully awake. He'd once heard a story about a man whose arm had fallen asleep and never come back. At one point the man begged his doctor to amputate the arm, saying that he couldn't take it anymore, the constant reminder was too much. Vaughn never knew the real ending to the story, only that the man apparently opted to keep the arm in a sling, telling people he had polio, in order to make sense of it.

He walked slowly down K Street, heading toward his office on Connecticut. Quiet streets. Quiet minds. The moment between amnesia and recall. It reminded him of car accident victims who have had all the memories shocked right out of them. Their stories are always more dramatic when told by others. That is, until they can appropriate the story as their own. They don't have the key details, only the momentary blurs or the song on the radio or the moment of waking up. Vaughn Ferguson was making sure that everything he would know of these days was clean. Traffic: not very much. Weather: cool and overcast. Streets: breathless and deserted. Washington: the color of the lawns; the pasty government buildings. And the sound of the wind. And the echoes of a hollow city. And the on and on and on. Mental pinches to tell himself he was not dreaming.

A gust of wind blew open his overcoat, and on the knee of his bum leg he saw a kernel of rose petal pressed into the wool. Probably picked up when he was kneeling to clean the buttons.

He reached down to pull the petal off his knee. A sniper wind took it from his hand. The petal skipped behind him. He stamped in awkward dance steps to catch it. A street performer alone in Federal Triangle. With the next squall, he lost sight of it altogether. He crouched. Lifted on his tiptoes. The breeze was making his eyes water. Warm tears traced down his cheeks. Far ahead on the sidewalk, alone along Connecticut Avenue and heading toward Pennsylvania, Vaughn Ferguson thought he caught sight of the rose petal pushing along the sidewalk. Confident. With purpose. Like it knew what it was doing. Where it was going. Where it was supposed to be.

Here are some final thoughts:

When J. Hyman wrote to President Johnson in January of 1964, he likely was expressing a sentiment that many others felt. Hyman—president of Unitron of California, a company that imported and manufactured home-improvement items, from bamboo shutters to plastic rakes—wanted to share his disappointment upon learning that the bubbletop limousine would be pressed back into service following a series of alterations and refurbishments. In his letter, Hyman praises Johnson for his ability to lead during such a trying time. But still, he questions the judgment of putting the car back into service. He asserts that the United States, being the richest country in the world, "which has some 80 million automobiles and trucks rolling along its highways, is entitled to a brand-new automobile, and should not be called upon to ride in the shadow of the world's most tragic incident that has occurred during the last twentieth century."

Ivan Sinclair, assistant to the president, signed the reply from the White House. On behalf of Johnson, Sinclair expressed his appreciation for Hyman's concern. He went on to explain that the Secret Service recommended continued use of the limousine, citing time as the main factor. "There are numerous special features in this vehicle," he writes, "and it would take several weeks—possibly even months—to construct another. Security requirements would not permit such a delay." He goes on to explain that more features would be added to enhance security, again, "with a minimum of delay."

Four months later, on April 27, Douglass Dillon, secretary of the treasury, sent a memo to Johnson informing the president that the modifications and repairs on the limousine were completed and the car would be delivered during the following month. He reiterated that the Secret Service made the recommendation, noting that with "recent advances in the field of armoring and glasswork, it was believed possible to reconstruct the top of the car so it would be both bulletproof and transparent." As an added feature, there would be an "opaque fabric cover" that could be fitted over the transparent top, allowing the retrofitted car to be used as either a parade car or a standard limousine. However, there was still concern from the Secret Service that the president understand that he needed to stay seated. As Special Agent Behn wrote in a communication whose tone sounds almost parental, "If the president was not agreeable to remaining seated in the car during the parade, it would be a waste of money and effort . . . to build these cars."

On June 12, Dillon writes Johnson to say that the rebuilt bubbletop was delivered the previous evening, ready for use. He personally inspected it and found the car to be "comfortable and conservative looking." Dillon tells the president that he does not expect "that it would draw any unusual attention by its appearance." At about this same time, Ford Motor Company, which headed the refurbishment, issues a press release announcing the return of the rebuilt "custom version of a 1961 Lincoln Continental [that] retains virtually the same appearance as it did when it was originally delivered to President John F. Kennedy in the spring of 1961." After explaining some of the changes, it informs the reader that the car was rebuilt both by Ford mechanics in Dearborn, Michigan, and in Cincinnati, Ohio, by Hess & Eisenhardt, the same custom-body firm that had been part of the team that originally built the car, in 1961. And in a strange conclusion to the press release, there is an almost upbeat and cheery call for process, telling the reader that revamping White House limousines "has been the rule rather than the exception." It then gives examples of three eras of cars—Roosevelt's, Truman's, and Eisenhower's—that had been refurbished and upgraded for various reasons.

But none because someone was murdered in its backseat.

When the new limousine was scheduled to be part of a presidential motorcade through Des Moines on October 7, 1964, Johnson's press people seemed to get a sudden shiver of concern about the perception of the car. The worry was that reporters would recognize the bubbletop, and they might bring up questions about employing it, regarding its history and such. Press Secretary George Reedy and his assistant, Dixon Donnelley, decide that the only information to be furnished to the media will be the press release issued by Ford Motors. Of course, if asked, they will confirm that it is indeed the bubbletop. However, the press secretary and his representatives will be limited to making the "following points: 1. That the President was using the car upon the direct order or urging of the President's Committee. 2. That in effect this was a brand new car."

Perhaps J. Hyman was listening to President Johnson's news conference on October 3, 1964. Johnson hadn't yet left for Des Moines. Hadn't yet sat in his brand-new car. A little after three, in the White House, Johnson is standing before the press pool. It is about midway through that he is asked about his response to the Warren Commission recommendations about safety, specifically whether those recommendations will affect Johnson's public style. And he sounds testy. He sounds bothered. It's clear he doesn't think any of the reporters fully understand the relationship between the expectations of a president's contact with the public versus policies and procedures. Then he challenges their reading of the recommendations and parses words such as *suggestion*, as opposed to *recommendation*. He cites the reports. Cites memos from the Secret Service. And in the end, he relays his trust in the Secret Service and its recommendations. "It is irritating to go in an old car that sometimes roars and you can't even talk in it," he states, "but if they recommend it, that is what we do."

Maybe J. Hyman is holding his breath, swallowing down every word. Perhaps in his office at Unitron in Hawthorne, California, he wants to throw open the window, lean his head out, and shout among the roar of the planes taking off and landing at nearby Los Angeles International Airport. Scream that history is not just a function of its parts, that you can pave over battlefields but that doesn't mean people never died there. You can order and reorder the words any way you want, but it can't change what it describes. He wants to scream until his voice is hoarse, until it becomes part of the history.

Instead, though, maybe he stays at his desk, clears his throat, and thumbs through the pages of the new Unitron catalog, looking at the garden tools he'll be exporting. He reviews page after page of rakes, waiting for the bamboo shutters, handling each sheet carefully, sensitive to how easily ink can smudge. Leaf rakes. Bow rakes. Sweep rakes. He turns each page slowly. When he reaches the end, he flips back to the beginning, trying not to think of a widow who didn't want to remove her bloodied dress, but once she did, and stood naked in front of a mirror, saw she was still stained.

Acknowledgments

While this book is written largely from imagination, valuable contributions from among the following cannot be dismissed: transcripts from the Warren Commission and the Assassination Records Review Board; the John F. Kennedy Presidential Library and Museum for its archives, helpful archivists, and specifically its Oral History collection, where the following transcripts were accessed: Kenneth Burke, David P. Highly, Jacqueline Kennedy Onassis, Nelson Pierce, Maud Shaw, Cordenia Thaxton, Nancy Tuckerman and Pamela Turnure, and J. Bernard West; the Lyndon B. Johnson Presidential Library and Museum; the White House Historical Foundation; the Museum of Broadcast Communications; the Sixth-Floor Museum at Dealey Plaza; the National Archives; the Assassination Archives and Research Center; the Smoking Gun; History.net; U.S. Army Center of Military History; Cornell Lab of Ornithology; the Handbook of Texas Online; the Henry Ford Museum; the American Presidency Project; American Radio Works; the *Washington Post*; the *New York Times*; the *Dallas Morning News*; *Time* magazine; CNN; PBS; *Vogue*; History Matters; U.S. Army Corps of

Engineers; Arlington National Cemetery; *The White House: An Historic Guide* (1963); Susan Bennett and Cathy Trust's *President Kennedy Has Been Shot*; James Fetzer's *Murder in Dealey Plaza*; Robert Drew's documentaries *Primary, Crisis,* and *Faces of November*; National Geographic's documentary *Air Force One*; CBS News' documentary *A Tour of the White House with Mrs. John F. Kennedy*; Bruce Halford's documentary *JFK: The Day the Nation Cried*; Bobby Hargis, Aubrey Rike, and James Tackach for being generous enough to tell their stories again; all of the Kennedy enthusiasts who have amassed and archived a wealth of unique, important information that is posted on the Internet—a special thanks to those who were willing to answer e-mails in the middle of the night.

I'm also grateful to all the good, dedicated folks at Tin House (Lee, Michelle, Meg, Deb, and others I don't even know yet); Nat and Judith, Julie Stevenson, and everyone else at Sobel Weber; friends and colleagues who acted as readers and sounding boards; Howard Norman for injecting confidence, and Amy Hempel for talking me back *onto* the ledge; Roy Nirschel and Bob Boyers for the gift of time; and of course Alisson, Addison, and the rest of my family for the certainty of unconditional love.

ALSO BY ADAM BRAVER

Mr. Lincoln's Wars
Divine Sarah
Crows Over the Wheatfield